Murder in Pigeon Cove

The Third Annie Quitnot Mystery

. . .

GUNILLA CAULFIELD

ISBN: 1461089735
ISBN-13: 9781461089735
LCCN: 2011905997

Also by Gunilla Caulfield:

FICTION:

Reunification Express

*

The Wave
A Novel in the Time of Global Warming

*

The Bookseller and Other Stories

* * *

MYSTERIES:

Murder on Bearskin Neck
(The first Annie Quitnot mystery)

*

Murder at Hammond Castle
(The second Annie Quitnot mystery)

DEDICATION:

To the hardy citizens of Pigeon Cove.

To June Sullivan, Rockport Outreach Librarian, who recently retired at age 90.

To all the libraries in my life, especially the city libraries of Solna and Stockholm, Sweden, where I grew up; the Boston Public Library, where I spent a lot of time during my first ten years in this country; the Newburyport Public Library in Massachusetts; the Bridgton Public Library in Maine, The Portsmouth Public Library in New Hampshire, and, most of all, the Rockport Public Library on Cape Ann, Massachusetts.

A thimble-ful about the Rockport Public Library:

This massive, gray granite structure—surely the heaviest building in Rockport—sits a block away from Sandy Bay, looking as indestructible as the pyramid of Giza. But looks can be deceiving, and the building has been through some trying times. It was originally built to house the Annisquam Steam Cotton Mill, a successful industrial venture for a small, rural village in the 1800's. The millworkers lived in a row of Corporation Houses on Broadway, directly across the street from the factory. However, after a devastating fire in the mill in December 1883, the factory closed, and the millworkers scrambled to get jobs elsewhere. The ruins, including a large fallen tower, left a scar on the center of town for many years. Finally, the tower was razed and the main structure rebuilt, serving for a time as a school. (The street is still known as School Street.) The millworkers' frugal habitations on Broadway have since been revamped into more upscale private homes, part of the gentrification process that is rampant along Boston's North Shore.

The *old* Rockport Public Library, the Carnegie—another solid granite building, one of many libraries made possible by Andrew Carnegie back in the day—was located around the corner on Jewett Street, just on the other side of the Congregational Church, or "the Congo Church," as it's known by the locals. When the librarians in the old Carnegie could no longer squeeze any more books onto its shelves, a generous benefactor named Franz Denghausen came to the town's aid, through a codicil in his will. Local architect Mallory Lash—named after the legendary Mt. Everest climber George Mallory, and himself a great adventurer in the Far East—oversaw the interior restructuring and design, and the new library was inaugurated in the old mill building in 1993. The library is a beacon that draws people into its light and warmth and bustle. Bustle isn't something normally found in libraries, but the Rockport Public Library is a different kind of place altogether.

• • •

Most of all, this book is lovingly dedicated to my family.

PROLOGUE

The year is coming to a close. Annie Quitnot, standing on the Headlands in the chill December air, will be glad to see it end. Annie looks out to sea, where white-caps eat away at the edges of the breakwater, far out in the bay, before chasing each other toward shore. Squawking seagulls battle the winds, rolling and gliding, to finally settle on a granite ledge down at the water's edge. Ten years ago, this is where Annie had stood, day after day, waiting for her parents to return from a pleasure trip in her father's small motorboat. She had lost all hope of ever seeing them again, but the sea sometimes divulges its secrets, and their bodies had finally been recovered. Annie still feels close to her parents here and often walks up to the Headlands when she has things to think about, which is the case today.

It has been a year of turmoil, beginning with the murder of Carlo Valenti. Annie and Carlo, a well known Rockport artist, had been lovers until Carlo suddenly decided to move to Rome. His going had left Annie devastated, putting her life on a standstill. With Carlo gone, the library had become Annie's salvation. Her position at the reference desk suited her perfectly, giving her totally engrossing tasks to fill her day. Then, after being gone for five years, Carlo had returned, just as suddenly as he had left—only to be brutally murdered. Annie had suddenly become the main suspect, and had been suspended from the library for a time. She still cringes at the memory. Annie's brother Justin had come to give his support and, to Annie's chagrin at the time, had hired the venerated Judge Bradley to defend her in the case. But that is all over now, and in the past.

After that, there was Duncan. Duncan Langmuir, the director of the library, had sensed early on what Annie was going through during Carlo's absence, and had been quietly supportive. After Carlo's death, Duncan had given Annie a gentle hint of his own feelings toward her, but it had been too early for her, and she had simply fled. Taking time off from the library to visit her brother in New Mexico had helped restore her equilibrium. For five years she had hoped for Carlo's return—now she was finally able to deal with the fact that he would never be back.

When she returned to work in the fall, Duncan had doggedly persisted in trying to win her affections, and Annie had been ready. Not only because, at forty, she was staring permanent spinsterhood in the eye, but mainly because she found that Duncan had somehow managed to worm his way into her heart.

The wedding at Hammond Castle had started as a dream and ended as a nightmare. A medieval feast, accompanied by music from Hammond's famous pipe organ, had been rudely followed by violent death. Annie, angered at the intrusion of murder at her wedding, had put her agitated brain to the test and even enlisted the help of the curmudgeonly Judge Bradley to solve the case. While the surprising conclusion had caused Annie some additional grief, life afterwards has seemed ever so rosy. The marriage experiment seems to be working out quite satisfactorily—the only sticking point being: *whose quarters will they choose to live in?* Duncan has his rather elegant Victorian domicile, which he is reluctant to give up; Annie has her own family home, an old clapboarded cottage that sits right on the harbor. So far, they are both hoping that their own abode will become their future home.

CHAPTER ONE

"Go little book! From this my solitude
I cast thee on the waters—go thy ways."
(Robert Southey, "Lay of the Laureate")

As usual, the circulation desk is busy during the first hour of the day. Library Assistant Jean Stokes has already filled two trolleys with returned books for the pages to shelve when they come in after school. She is working on the third, slapping each book down on the metal trolley with a light thwacking sound, when she stops for a moment to fix a pin that has come loose on her collar, a little bouquet of violets glistening with tiny amethysts. Before she returns to her chore, she takes a small bite of a candy bar and slips the rest into her pocket. Seeing a young patron approaching the desk with a load of books, Jean immediately steps up to the computer to check them out, swallowing the last of her snack quickly. Jean knows the boy's mother, Lorraine Davis, and wants no trouble with the son. Lorraine had Jean figured long ago as the weakest of the desk set, and takes cruel advantage of her, getting out of paying fines or being allowed to take out more books than allowed on a current subject.

Jean makes a mistake on the keyboard, blushes, corrects the mistake, and finally puts the date-due slips inside the books and passes them across the desk.

"There you go, Tim, have a nice day," she says, giving him a nervous smile. She remembers to call him Tim, and not Timmy, according to Lorraine's recent instructions.

Marie Stewart, head of circulation, is busy at her computer slogging her way through interlibrary loan requests, entering them methodically from a fat wad of pink slips while mumbling wearily that it would be nice if more patrons would make the requests online, preferably from home. She heaves a sigh, squinting at the screen. Marie has never bothered to get computer-distance glasses and must lean forward in order to read the screen. Most staff members have a couple of different pairs of glasses dangling on their chests—a must for librarians past middle age, in order to read the book spines on the top shelf as well as the text of a book held in the hand. And those progressive glasses just won't do, what with running up and down the stairs all day.

Stupefied into a trance of concentration, and with her back turned, Marie is blissfully unaware that Jean is collapsing behind her in the enclosure created by the main desk. The slender assistant simply floats to the ground, making no more sound than a sheet of paper would, landing softly on the rubber-backed carpet. Sensing the sudden silence, however—*what happened to the thwacks?*—Marie turns around. She utters a small shriek, certainly unexpected from this particular librarian, who is usually imperturbable.

• • •

After a gale that had petered out the night before, it's turned into one of those late fall days when nature seems to hold its breath—as if that could stave off winter. It's futile in the end, of course. The return of nature's breath will arrive suddenly from the north, loaded with sharp needles, a warning of change. In New England, early fall is a glorious riot of color, but late fall is a bleak season of black and brown and wine. Tangy winds come whooshing in from the sea, encrusting the windows with salt in a grim foreshadowing of soon-to-come frosts. Leaves, thick and hard after a summer of alternating drought and torrential downpours, flop like old leather gloves onto green lawns, where they stubbornly refuse to break down. Maple leaves have *tar spots* this year and must be raked up and dealt with severely to prevent them from spreading the nasty fungus next year. Anxious starlings gather and swarm in the sky. Like schools of fish they soar and turn in huge amorphous clouds continually changing shape. Suddenly, as if on cue, they descend and spread out in neat rows on telephone wires. There they sit, their fat little bodies equidistant, as if measured by a ruler, chattering and squeaking noisily until one starts up and leads them away in another wild dance.

Annie Quitnot, the reference librarian, daydreams at her desk, spinning slowly in her leather chair, watching the dance of the dust-motes tumbling in the sunbeams. The sun makes her Irish red hair gleam as she pulls it back and twirls it into a tight knot at the nape of her neck. It stays put of its own volition, stubborn curls grabbing each other like cockleburs.

The work pile on the reference desk is daunting. School projects are due, and Thanksgiving is coming soon. Not a time for daydreams. She pushes the stack aside, taking a temporary break from processing reference requests, and checks her notepad. Next on the day's general task list is one of her favorites: the weekly "stumper." She started posting this quiz page on the wall by the main desk years ago to give patrons something to do while waiting in line. Next week she will post the solution, along with the names of the first three patrons who got it right.

• • •

THIS WEEK'S STUMPER
What do these book titles have in common?
Brave New World
Remembrance of Things Past
Band of Brothers
The Sound and the Fury
The Dogs of War
Something Wicked this Way Comes
Cakes and Ale
Please leave your answers in the purple folder!
Have fun! Annie

• • •

Just as she finishes, Annie hears the stifled cry. She doesn't see anyone at the main desk and wonders where the sound has come from. Suddenly, Marie's anxious face rears up into view, flushed after being bent over whatever is down there on the floor. Marie is of a rather substantial build—still, out of respect and fondness, no one would ever think of commenting on her amplitude. Annie hurries over and sees Jean's inert body on the floor.

"Oh, what happened?"

"I didn't see…I just felt the whoosh of her dress, and then it got quiet. She isn't coming to. I tried giving her arm a squeeze. We'd better call an ambulance."

Marie bends down again, speaking softly to Jean, who lies there looking like a giant praying mantis—legs bent and arms held in a beseeching gesture. As befits a dedicated librarian, she is still grasping a book in one hand. Annie picks it up—*Beautiful Lies*—and sticks it on the trolley on the way to the desk, where she hits the local emergency button on the phone.

Annie and Marie kneel beside the inert body.

"What can be wrong? She seemed fine a few minutes ago. Just fainted, you think?" Marie asks anxiously. Patrons are beginning to gather around the desk, curious and anxious. Marie asks them to move aside to leave room for the emergency crew. The sirens can be heard outside already.

EMTs arrive and quickly check on Jean's condition before strapping her to a gurney. As the gurney passes by, Marie pulls Jean's purple dress down over her knees. Jean would appreciate the gesture; she wouldn't want to be carried out of the library with her knobby knees exposed.

Duncan Langmuir, the library's director, who hurried down from his office as soon as Annie buzzed him on the intercom, now follows the crew out to the ambulance, buttoning his tweed jacket to ward off the chill. When he returns, all who have gathered around the desk look at him, their faces tight with worry.

"What did they say?" Annie asks.

"Just that she's unconscious," Duncan replies. Well, they all knew that.

"We must call her husband." Marie says, suddenly alert.

"Come up to my office then, Marie. You are closer to Jean than anyone else here, and I'm sure it would be a comfort for her husband to hear from you first. Then I'd like to talk to him myself, to tell him where Jean has been taken, and so on."

CHAPTER TWO

"Speak to me as to thy thinkings,
As thou dust ruminate, and give thy worst of thoughts
The worst of words."
(Shakespeare, Othello)

Annie reluctantly takes up the watch at the main desk, waiting for Marie to come back down from Duncan's office. Tonight is Library Coffee night, with Annie's turn to host it, and the cupboard is bare. She usually gets out at five on Thursdays and had planned to do some shopping for the event, but now time is running short, and she finds herself checking her watch in agitation every few minutes. Marie finally appears, shaking her head in obvious frustration.

"We couldn't get hold of Brian. We have no record of his work number, so Duncan had to leave a message on their home phone. Isn't that awful? Don't know who else to call—as far as I know, she has no other family around here. Poor Jean…I do hope she's awake by now. Duncan called the hospital, but they won't give him any information. He's not *next of kin*, you know," Marie says, wagging her head from side to side in disgust. Annie sighs.

"You know, I can't believe that she just fainted. She would have come to more quickly, don't you think? There's got to be something else wrong…" Annie bites her lip, pondering.

"Oh, Annie, let's not start speculating," Marie sounds distressed. *I wish Annie would stick to dealing with reference questions,* she thinks, but she knows that Annie has a one-track mind when it comes to solving mysteries.

"They wouldn't be so tight-lipped if there wasn't something suspicious about the whole thing," Annie insists sullenly. "Anyway, the hospital staff must have a way of reaching her husband. Jean's been living in Rockport long enough. They must have her on file...you know, health care proxy, that kind of thing. Sometimes," Annie adds, "I think they carry that privacy thing too far."

"I agree. The proxy would be Brian, so I'm sure they've tried to get hold of him. How about if you and I go over to the hospital later to see if we can visit? Hopefully she'll be awake by then." Marie, ever practical, is trying to keep things simple. To her, there seems to be no reason to panic. Surely Jean will have come to by the time they get to the hospital.

"Good idea. I'll pick you up as soon as Duncan and I have had supper. I'm going to the store right now; I'll make sure to get something that'll cook up quick." Of course, anything Annie cooks has to be quick, her cooking motto being *half an hour max from grocery bag to table.*

When Annie and Marie arrive at the ward, they are told that no visitors are allowed. Only family members will be admitted. Annie tries to find out whether Brian or any other family member has actually been reached, but the desk nurse simply asks them to return tomorrow.

"We're just worried about our colleague. Can you just tell us if she's awake yet?" Marie asks.

"Why don't you give us a call in the morning? I'm sure we'll know more by then," the nurse says, with a bureaucratic smile that does not reach her sea-blue eyes, before turning back to her computer.

"Cold fish," Annie says when they get out into the corridor."See what I mean, though? Tell me honestly, don't you think there's something fishy about the way they're stonewalling us?"

"Oh, it's only rules, just like we have at the library. Privacy. Claptrap. I'm sure the insurance companies have something to do with it, and the lawyers, too." Marie likes to lay the blame of most of society's ills on insurance companies and lawyers. It's a recurring theme—a favorite townie rant, actually, along with harping on other globally important issues put forth by the townies, the likes of *resident parking* and *selling off town land to expand the tax base.*

It's Annie turn to be eager to change the subject. Though born and raised in Rockport, she has never been fond of the townie rant.

"Well, I'm getting worried, now," she says. "Are they just going to let her lie there? What if she needs some emergency treatment, but they can't get hold of Brian? Let's drive by Jean's house, just in case he's come home."

"Let's do." Marie nods.

Jean lives in Pigeon Cove, a section of Rockport on the northern end of the island of Cape Ann. Annie knows it well, having spent most of her childhood in the Cove. Back then, the Quitnot family had lived in an old house overlooking Pigeon Cove Harbor, just next to the old Tool Company, where Annie's father had been working. Her mother, Mairead, had been the Pigeon Cove branch librarian and had taught Annie the rudiments of library science, without ever knowing what it would lead to.

Keystone Bridge takes them into Pigeon Cove. The "Covers" consider this crossing something akin to the *Great Divide* between themselves and the rest of Rockport—and the rest of the world, for that matter. They are an independent lot and don't generally even own to being Rockporters. Continuing northward, Granite Street follows the curve of Sandy Bay. At the very tip of Pigeon Cove lies Halibut Point, a wild and rocky place with a large, water filled quarry; a heath overgrown with blueberries, huckleberries, and cat briar; and a promontory with a fine view of the coastlines of Massachusetts, New Hampshire and Maine. Along the road they ride past some of the larger homes of the Cove, expensive residences perched high above the water's edge, where their owners can feel safe from hurricanes and still enjoy vast and wild ocean views. Shortly after passing the high point called Pigeon Hill, they turn left onto Old Quarry Lane, one of the long, winding roads that lead to the edge of Dogtown, the forested wilderness that occupies the center of the island.

The Stokes' home, Annie realizes, lies not far from where her old friend Josie Mandel used to live before she moved in with Judge Bradley—an event that had caused a ripple of whispered comments among the gossip squad in town. After all, Judge and Josie were...well, elderly. But, in time, the whispers had died down, Judge being one of the most respected men in Rockport. In fact, Judge had given Annie away at her wedding in Hammond Castle, and Annie smiles at the memory. Judge and Josie have since become Annie's and Duncan's close friends, and Annie feels a guilty stab. She must call Josie soon and arrange for a get-together.

"It's too dark on this road at night. I can't believe they have no streetlights up here," Marie complains.

Annie nods, but speeds up anyway in order to get past Mrs. Ridley's cottage, where the lights are on in the living room. Reflections from a TV flicker on the walls. Mrs. Ridley is an old nemesis of Annie's. Annie knows that the woman had a lot to do with her suspension from the library during the investigation of Carlo's murder. Mrs. Ridley had enjoyed painting Annie as a likely suspect as soon as word was leaked in the *Cape Ann Chronicle* that Annie and Carlo had been lovers in the past.

Annie pulls into the Stokes' driveway. It's a solitary place with no other houses within view. The rambling ranch house sits back a little in the spacious yard, surrounded by old shade trees and shrubs. The back end of the property borders on the wild woods of Dogtown—in fact, a footpath leads from the yard into the woods through a stand of old hemlocks before it divides into separate trails. One trail leads to a group of water-filled granite quarries; another winds its way toward Whale's Jaw, an aptly descriptive name for a couple of great rocks deposited by the glacier long ago. Standing to an impressive height, they had looked like a giant whale with its jaw open to feed, but that was before some brainless hiker built a fire underneath them, which cracked the jaw. Now the poor whale has finished feeding, the bottom of half of his big jaw lying flat on the ground—all the better to sit on while munching on a few blueberries.

Tall spruces grow in a row along the fence on the street side of Jean's house, effectively shielding the house and yard from passersby. The sugar maples in the side yard have lost their brilliant fall mantles and are outlined starkly against a moonlit sky. As they pull up next to the house, motion-activated lights come on, illuminating the front steps and the two garage doors. The house itself lies in darkness. They get out and Annie knocks on the wooden door, but there is no response. Annie peers into the garage. In the faint light she can see two empty bays. Annie makes a mental note to call her friend Billy Hale at the police department to make sure Jean doesn't get a ticket for leaving her car in the library lot overnight.

"No cars. Guess he isn't home," Annie says.

"He takes the train. Maybe he leaves the car at the train station. You know, Brian may not come back tonight. Sometimes he's gone for long stretches." Marie pulls a tissue from her coat pocket and blows her nose. The evening is getting chilly, and she shivers. "Let's go or I'll catch a cold."

They hurry back to the car and get in, casting a last glance toward the house. No lights come on inside as Annie starts the car and backs out of the driveway.

"What does he do?" Annie puts on the highbeams as she winds her way downhill.

"Works for the government. CIA or FBI, I heard someone say, but that may just be talk. You know how it is. I don't know her all that well; we just go out for coffee or a walk sometimes. Just talk about the library mostly, books or patrons or upcoming events, nothing personal. I wouldn't say she's secretive, exactly, but the Stokes are private people. I've known Jean for years, but not well enough to say we're *friends*. I don't think Jean has any close friends, at least she's never mentioned anyone that I remember. I'm surprised she even comes to our Library Coffee night."

"Funny you should say that," Annie says as she turns the heat on in the car, "that's the only time I ever hear her come out with a personal opinion. She hardly ever talks about herself. Tough childhood, maybe? And in the library she'll just agree with whatever anyone says. She'll never correct the kids, even when they have the wrong author; she'll just go and get them the right book off the shelf and hand it to them. I know...I know...we're not supposed to be their teachers, but still. Well, Jean won't be coming to coffee tonight, will she? Oh, boy, I've got you lot coming over in a little while, don't I? I guess we should be speeding up."

Annie drives through the darkened Pigeon Cove, back across Keystone Bridge and on to her house in downtown Rockport, carelessly doing a bit above the maximum 20 past the post office and the fire station. The new police station complex has moved over to Great Hill now, the better to catch speeders coming into town. It's quite a change from the small wing attached to the rear of the fire station that until recently housed the local constabulary.

"Come on in and stick around until the rest of them show up," Annie urges, eager to get the place in order.

CHAPTER THREE

"Sleep not, dream not; this bright day
Will not, cannot last for aye;
Bliss like thine is brought by years
Dark with torment and with tears."
(Emily Bronte, "Sleep Not")

Jean lies motionless in her hospital bed, showing no signs of regaining consciousness. Jumbled images from the past appear on her secret dream screen. Dreams, memories...Do any of the images cause a disturbance, deep down in her unconscious? Her hands lie perfectly still on the white hospital sheet. The monitor shows no sign of what's going on inside her mind. Her face is marble, not a tic or flutter reveals the upheaval inside.

The gigantic shapes of her parents hover over her, Mama full of thunder, as usual, and Papa spreading his lovely summer warmth. Eventually, her parents float away and are replaced by Brian—a young, sunny-faced Brian, with a glory of dark, curly hair. Here he is, so vividly alive, with a red carnation...no, it was a geranium... behind his ear. He is doing a dance, trying to look like José Greco, stepping wildly to an imagined flamenco, stomping his heel, tapping his toe, clapping his hands rhythmically. The scene switches, and now they are in Brian's dorm room, listening to his portable record player. Frank Sinatra is singing "Night and Day." The sound bounces off the walls in that little cubbyhole of a room. The record is scratched, being one of their favorites. They get up and dance, his arm is tight around her waist. There is only room for a step or two in any direction, and finally they stumble and flop down on the bed, laughing.

Another image takes over, and the visual tempo speeds up. The subconscious knocks on the door of the conscious as her blood warms to the memories. Suddenly, the dream takes a different turn, and she cringes inwardly. Something alerts her that she had better remain down in the murk, not rise up to the surface. There is danger in consciousness. Fearfully, instinctively, she clings to the darkness.

CHAPTER FOUR

"Unbidden guests
Are often welcomest when they are gone."
(Shakespeare, King Henry VI)

Duncan is sitting in his favorite chair reading the newspaper. He has changed into his after-work uniform: corduroys and an Irish cardigan that's a bit worn at the elbows, but still comfortable. Annie sends him upstairs until the rest of the librarians arrive, and tells him to get some peace and quiet before what usually turns into a spirited discussion. Then she starts the coffee, while Marie helps empty the dishwasher so there will be enough cups.

"I can't stop worrying about poor Jean. You know, she never complains. She hasn't changed much since I first met her." Marie looks fretful.

"She's been here a long time, but I know she's not from here. Wonder how she got her job to start with." Annie sets out a tray for the cups and silverware.

"She started out as a volunteer, like you, and then she worked as a substitute until she got her fulltime job. But when the trustees offered to help pay for her getting an MLS, she turned them down. Said she didn't want a job with too much responsibility. I think she's sorry now. She's still shy, but she has more self-confidence, and she's much smarter than people think. Maybe, like you say, she had a tough childhood, or it was just the way she was brought up...you know, maybe her parents were very strict. My guess is that she probably never even finished high school, but was afraid to tell the trustees."

Marie grabs a towel and wipes the dishes dry, remembering that Annie has the virtuous habit of trying to save energy by not using the drying cycle.

"I know Stuart gives her a hard time," Annie says with a wry smile, "'*The meek one,*' he calls her. He's relentless once he finds someone to pick on, and Jean's such easy prey." Annie is referring to Stuart Cogswell, the supercilious and ever-reluctant children's librarian, who is constantly angling for a position with more status—director, head librarian, even reference librarian would do fine—anything to get him out of the children's room and the job he considers beneath him.

"Oh, I know. She doesn't get hurt as easily as she once did, though. I remember when she used to hide in the dungeon and have a cry every time Stuart put her down." Marie shakes her head at the memory. "Now, Annie, go get Duncan," she begs, when Maureen and Clare arrive. Maureen, the elderly outreach librarian, is bringing something home-baked wrapped in foil.

"But, Maureen, it isn't your turn!"

"Oh, you know I love to bake. And I was minding the grandchildren, so I had to be around anyway."

They hang their coats on the hooks in the hall. Maureen comes into the kitchen to find a plate for her cake, and Annie puts her own store-bought cookies back in the cupboard. The door opens, and Geri, Duncan's assistant, walks in, a little out of breath.

"Am I late? I hope I didn't keep you. This having a day off in the middle of the week is the pits. Got stuck in traffic on Route 1, just by the shopping malls. You'd think Christmas was next week."

"You're not the last. Stuart's not here yet," Annie says.

They sit down and wait for Cogswell, who has consistently been the last to arrive lately. Annie takes a turn around the room with the coffee pot.

"So, Marie, does Brian work out-of-state?" she asks, trying to get back to their previous topic, while topping Marie's cup.

"I think so. He spends a lot of time wherever it is he goes. Jean said he has a small efficiency apartment somewhere near his workplace. When he does come home, he and Jean usually go away—up the coast somewhere. They have a camp in New Hampshire or Maine…Rye, maybe, or Hampton, some place like that."

"Ogunquit," Maureen says, smiling, fluffing her white curls gently. "I sub for Jean sometimes, you know, and she's told me they go up to their camp in Ogunquit."

"Brian never shows his face in town. I've asked them over for dinner or coffee a few times, but Jean always politely says no. She says that whenever Brian comes home he's too exhausted to socialize. So, I've stopped asking." Marie leans back in her chair, which creaks ominously in protest.

"What if her husband's up there? At the camp, I mean," Annie quickly grasps at a new straw.

"Oh, I don't think so. It's closed up for the winter," Maureen says, unwrapping her coffeecake and cutting it into thick slices. "The camp isn't heated; it's just a small summer cottage in somebody's backyard. They rent the same one every year, I guess."

Duncan comes down, yawning and sleepy-eyed, just as the children's librarian turns up. Stuart quickly eyes the available seating. A timely arrival, since it gives him a choice—Duncan and Annie are still on their feet, and Jean, of course, isn't present. He suspiciously scans the unoccupied seats. Annie's furniture is comfortably worn and well-camouflaged with spreads, quilts, and paisley shawls. Who knows what wicked springs might attack from the rear, or what smelly dog hairs might attach themselves to one's person? With an audible sigh of pleasure, Stuart sinks down into Duncan's leather wing chair. It's one of the few pieces that Duncan has brought with him to Annie's house. Duncan accepts the loss with equanimity, and he and Annie squeeze into her shredded brocade love seat, to sit squelched among a flurry of pillows and afghans. Eager fingers reach for Maureen's German coffeecake.

Marie finally manages to ask Duncan if he's gotten a substitute for Jean, and when he assures her that it's been taken care of, she sits back, sighing contentedly. Covering the main desk without help can be a daunting prospect.

"I suppose I've just missed all the news. How's the shrinking violet?" Stuart leans back, carefully scrutinizing the lip of his coffee mug for traces of lipstick or other unhygienic residue.

"If you mean Jean, we don't know yet." There is ice in Marie's voice.

"And what about Stokes, then, the errant husband, I guess he hasn't showed up either?" Stuart selects and jiggles out a middle slice of the coffeecake, where it would be least likely to have been fingered by anyone.

"It's odd to think that someone could live in Rockport that long without knowing anyone," Annie says. "Or want to, for that matter. Jean does seem lonely sometimes. Do you think... maybe her husband could be in a witness protection program or something?" Annie has always had a fanciful imagination. Her mother, being the realist in the family, had tried to cure her of it, but her father had only laughed. *"Let the child have her fantasies. She'll wake up to reality soon enough."* Apparently, it isn't soon enough yet. "I mean, you hear of people who are forced to do that, disappear into some safe community where they're not recognized," Annie goes on, warming to the idea.

Duncan tries to stop her from rattling on by jabbing her in the side. She jabs him right back. Marie shakes her head.

"Oh, I don't think so, Annie. Wouldn't be likely to hold a government job then, would he? And that much I heard from Jean herself, she just wasn't specific as to precisely what he does. She said Brian had been in the Navy. Went to Grenada. After that, he got a government desk job of some sort. Don't know if his current job is connected with the Navy. Could be he just works for the good old IRS."

"He went to Grenada? Maybe he was wounded. Disfigured, I mean. Something that could have made him people-shy." Annie continues her lonely quest for the truth, and Duncan resorts to stepping on her foot. She looks at him with raised eyebrows. "What? Do you have a better idea?"

"I think we're going a bit far afield here, Annie," Marie says firmly. "And as far as that bit about the FBI or CIA...well, you know how some people are around here. Runaway imaginations. It may just be talk."

"It *is* hard to imagine our timid little Jean being married to some kind of spy or secret agent."

Stuart lets out a guffaw at his own cleverness, scattering crumbs all over himself in his mirth.

Duncan picks up the coffeepot. "Warm-up, anyone? Let's change the subject. We have a lot to talk about. We'll start with holiday decorations. Any ideas?"

"Mrs. Sibley volunteered to do a Thanksgiving display in the children's room. Carved pumpkins, corn dolls, paper turkeys and so on." Marie avoids looking at Stuart.

"Dear God. Can't we dispense with all that?" Stuart shudders. "Last year one of the pumpkins rotted and stank up the place..."

"Well, Stuart, I'll ask Mrs. Sibley to talk to you, and you can set some rules. Everything to be made out of paper, or something like that. But our volunteers are important to the library. I don't want anyone to feel slighted." Duncan looks at the others. "Any other ideas? Christmas, Kwanzaa, Hanukkah?"

"Lorraine Davis offered to decorate the Christmas tree, if we're going to have one." Marie says, purposely avoiding Annie's eye.

Annie sighs. The Christmas tree is always placed in the reference area. While she enjoys the cheery lights and does not at all mind a bevy of excited kids running around jingling the bells on the tree, Annie has over the years developed a painful allergy to Lorraine Davis.

"Nothing religious, remember? We had some complaints last year." Duncan cautions.

"You mean the objections to the angels." Stuart looks heavenward.

"Yes. There can be no angels. Multicultural decorations, but no religious symbols. We'll have to vet the tree, but *politely.* And no volunteer is to do anything that requires ladders. Esa and I will put up the garlands. Annie says she will take care of Kwanzaa and Hanukkah, unless someone turns up to volunteer for that." As they assign decoration duties and other jobs, Clare speaks up for the first time.

"I'll be glad to help." Clare looks at Annie, as if she has to get her approval. Annie nods. The two women have more or less patched up their long friendship—they had gone to school together in Pigeon Cove—which had been strained after Carlo's death. Clare and Stuart had both believed Annie guilty of Carlo's murder, a fact that still sticks in Annie's craw. The two had also been in a relationship at the time, which Annie definitely couldn't understand. When that ended, Clare had fallen for a library trustee. That involvement, like many of Clare's previous love affairs, had also come to an abrupt finish.

Clare may be good with animals, but when it comes to men, her judgment is abominable, Annie thinks.

"Well, friends, it's been a long day," says Duncan, rising, and the guests take the hint and disappear into the chilly night. Winter's just around the corner.

Annie's venerable dachshund Gussie, named *Augustus Finknottle* after one of Annie's favorite characters in Jeeves and Wooster, has slept through the entire visit. Now he wakes up, sniffs the air, and rolls out of his basket. His elderly, well-hardened claws make a skrit-skrit noise on the wooden floor as he ambles over to his feeding station. *Ho-hum.* Nothing special there for him tonight, despite the party. There's a trail of crumbs along the floor, however, which his rheumy little eyes have discovered. He licks them up and smacks his lips, contemplating. *Blah. Not too exciting. Well, back to bed, one needs one's rest, after all.*

"Wonder what Stuart's up to that's so important he has to be late for coffee every week?" Annie is undressing to get into the shower.

"I guess I forgot to mention it," Duncan says, airily. "A while back, Stuart asked the trustees to pay for some courses. Working on another degree, I guess. That's why he's late every time, coming straight from class. Should be almost done, actually.."

"Wow. Does that mean he plans to move on? What a lovely turn of events that would be."

"Don't get your hopes up, Annie."

CHAPTER FIVE

"A room without books is like a body without a soul.
(Attributed to Cicero)

Annie takes her shower and goes to join Duncan in bed, but he isn't there. She finds him downstairs, sprawled on the worn old couch in the lower part of the living room. The picture window at the end wall overlooks the southern section of the inner harbor, which is split in half by T Wharf. The Sandy Bay Yacht Club, a rambling wooden structure of sun-bleached clapboard and shingles, takes up a large part of the wharf. To the left of the yacht club is the fishermen's loading area, with its rusty old crane used to haul lobster and crab pots. Plunked in the middle of the wharf is a big mooring stone for people to rest on—that is, if they can stand the smell of the lobster pots and aren't worried about sitting in seagull poop. The rest of the wharf is a parking lot shared by fishermen, tourists, yachtsmen, and residents—not always a good-natured blend. The fishermen feel they are the natural owners of the wharf, Rockport being an old fishing village. The summer tourists park anywhere, reasoning that any parking ticket they might get is cheaper than most all-day parking lot fees anywhere else. The yachtsmen insist there aren't enough spaces allotted to them along the fence of the yacht club, and the taxpaying local residents squawk all season long about the mainlanders who nonchalantly usurp all the "residents parking only" spots.

The Yacht Club is a busy place in the summertime, with a mix of seasoned yachtsmen and Sunday sailors scurrying around trying to get their boats in the water. The lights are on out there tonight, even though the sailing season is long since over. Diehard sailors still like to meet and swap yarns. They walk about in the Club Room, catching another look at the photos from the annual regatta before moseying outside to check up on the turnabouts and other small craft stored on the Yacht Club deck for the winter.

It's a calm night after last night's blow, and the placid black water mirrors the moon. Only workboats are left in the harbor now: a score of small lobster boats and a steadily shrinking number of larger fishing vessels. The fishermen are selling out. The government has set an even tighter restriction for the Massachusetts fishermen. Fishing is now restricted to twenty-four days a year. Not enough to pay for fuel, never mind a living.

Gussie is snuffling in his basket by the fireplace, probably put out because no one has built him a fire. Annie puts some crumpled newspaper, kindling, and a couple of logs on the grate and strikes a match. Gussie's eyes open for a split second before closing again. *Well, about time.*

Duncan is sleeping, too. Annie studies the long, ascetic shape of him. Argyle-stockinged feet stick out beyond the sofa. He looks younger, sleeping. That worried wrinkle between the eyebrows has been smoothed out. The auburn hair, silvery at the temples, is getting a bit shaggy, she thinks. Time for another attack with the shears. She leans over the back of the sofa and gives him an amorous kiss on the mouth, then hurries off before he has a chance to grab her. He catches up with her, of course, and, for a while at least, all's well with the world.

Once they are again installed in the living room, Annie sighs as she sinks down into the sofa with a cup of espresso that Duncan has prepared in the *galley*, as he refers to her tiny kitchen. A wrinkled linen pantsuit has replaced the almost identical, but slightly less wrinkled version that is her usual library wear. To Annie, wrinkles mean comfort. She slips out of her flip-flops, and they join another pair under the sofa—one of many pairs she keeps handy around the house.

"I hope that sigh was an expression of contentment." There is a small question in his voice.

"Naturally, Dunc. Although, now that you sort of brought it up, I must admit I'm still upset by all that happened today. It's so unsettling not to know what's wrong with Jean. Could it be something serious, like a heart attack or a stroke, or what? Other than a concussion from the fall, I can't imagine what else it could be. And the floor isn't that hard. And if she fell, what would have caused the fall? There was nothing there to trip on. And then, afterwards, for us not to be able to reach Brian…and maybe worst of all, finding out how little any of us know about Jean after all these years. It makes me feel kind of sad. She must have family somewhere, aside from her husband."

"Yes. I was surprised when I looked into her file and there was nothing much there. No CV with the salient facts—I guess, since she came up through the ranks after being a volunteer, it was never necessary. Brian's listed on her job application form, of course, but his employment information wasn't filled in at the time. Someone else, it must be one of the old trustees, simply penciled in 'Government' as his employer. I don't know offhand who the trustees were back then, or if they're still around. I suppose we could look into that, if it becomes necessary. They would have interviewed Jean at the time. I'll check with the current trustees. Maybe they know more about her than what's in the file. I was surprised, too. I was hoping that Marie would have some idea. She seems to be the one who knows her best. I don't even know where Jean's from, originally."

"Oh, but I do!" Annie's face lights up. "I remember that she once asked me for a pin, so I got her a pushpin from the drawer, and she said, 'No, no, a pin, you know, a ballpoint pin,' and I laughed. And then I asked her where she was from, and she said she and her husband both came from Tennessee. Something-ville...Louisville, I think she said, a small town. Not the Louisville in Kentucky, I remember she said it was in Tennessee. Where's my atlas?" Annie goes and pulls her atlas from the bottom shelf. "Yes, see, it's this little town, here. Oh, that gives me an idea. I'll go online and see if I can locate anyone in Brian's family there. They'd know how to get in touch with him, I'm sure."

"Hold on, hold on...please wait until tomorrow. Maybe Brian will be back by then, or the hospital may have reached him," Duncan pleads, reaching a hand out to hold her back. However, he knows it is fruitless to try to stop Annie once she has a notion. He had been fully aware of her obsessive personality even before their wedding. *Was it really possible that they had gotten married only just over a month ago?* They had agreed to accept and forgive each other's foibles, being mature people—some would even say middle-aged, but Annie, at forty, cringes at that—and each has an impressive list of well-ingrained habits and unique eccentricities. As Duncan well knows, one of Annie's traits is her obsession with *looking things up,* another, her often reckless impulsiveness. The first one stands her in good stead at her desk, while the second one worries him, sometimes.

"I'll just have a look. Won't hurt—you know, in case they don't get hold of him."

They settle for that, and Annie hurries to her old alcove bedroom, where she still keeps her computer. Duncan and Annie are living in *her* house for the month, her house being the old Hannah Jumper House, where Annie has lived since the family moved out of Pigeon Cove. Hannah Jumper was the famous—or, to some, infamous—woman who made Rockport a dry town, and that piece of history makes Annie feel that it is incumbent upon her, living in Hannah's own house, to vote *no* every time the liquor vote comes up and to celebrate with a glass of wine every time the proposition is defeated.

The house sits right on the main harbor, and Annie is panic-stricken at the thought of having to give the place up. They had tried Duncan's house for the first month. At the end of the trial, they are going to decide which one to keep and which to sell. In the beginning, they had both been stubborn and contentious, each trying to prove that his or her home was the more suitable. It had seemed an insurmountable hurdle, but Annie is starting to feel that she is winning Duncan over... so long as they can occupy her *whole* house, that is, and not rent out the studio apartment.

The studio is a small structure built onto the original house. Attached to the studio is a lean-to garage—*lean-to* describing it very well, as the whole thing leans precariously and gives Duncan the willies. In fact, Annie's car used to get stuck under the garage door until she had the door nailed permanently open.

Duncan has made a number of little sketches of what he might like to do with the studio addition...should they decide to live in Annie's house, of course. Most of his ideas have to do with covering every inch of wall space in the studio with bookshelves, since all the shelves in the main house are filled with Annie's collection. And no *weeding* goes on in her household; every book of Annie's is precious and not to be parted with. Duncan naturally feels the same about his own extensive cumulation, and once they have figured out which house will hold the most books, that is probably where they will settle.

Annie finds a few hits on Stokes in Louisville, prints them, stuffs the list into her jacket pocket and goes to bed. Naturally, she fully *intends* to honor her agreement with Duncan, and not make any calls until he gives her the go-ahead. When she finally crawls into bed, Duncan is snoring. She gives him a suggestive nudge to let him know she has other ideas. He groans, and rolls over reluctantly.

"Again?"

Half awake, he puts his hand on her hip and pulls her close.

CHAPTER SIX

"An empty house is like a stray dog or a body from which life has departed."
(Samuel Butler, The Way of All Flesh)

"See you in a bit, Dunc. Marie and I are driving by Jean's house to see if Brian is back, and then we're going to the coffee shop for a *cuppa* before work."

"Don't do anything...well, never mind. You know what I mean." A resigned note creeps into Duncan's voice.

"Who...me? Not to worry."

The sun has come out again, the second day in a row. Will wonders never cease? The air is quite balmy, in fact, must be in the mid-forties. Well, at least that's considered balmy in New England in November. Old Quarry Lane is much more pleasant in the early morning light; the yards are neat and woodsy, the houses modest but well kept. The road winds slowly uphill, eventually petering out somewhere past the Stokes' house. There it turns into a dirt trail, which joins the path into Dogtown that leads out from Jean's back yard. The properties along the road are of generous proportions, and large, mature shade trees surrounding the houses indicate that most of the homes up here were built a long time ago. Annie and Marie stop at the Stokes' again to see if Brian has returned. There is still no car in the garage.

"Is there a kitchen entrance at the back? Let's go check and make sure it's locked. With neither of them around, it wouldn't do to have a door unlocked," Annie says. She used to leave her own kitchen door unlocked, as many people still do in small New England towns. While Annie had been hiding out after Carlo's murder, that was how an intruder had once managed to get in and nearly kill Gussie. Annie shudders, remembering.

The kitchen door is indeed unlocked, and Annie opens it wide enough to peer inside.

"Halloo, anybody home? Brian, are you here?" she calls, but there is no answer.

Marie is starting to squirm. "Come on, Annie. We should go."

"Wait, I see a phone over there. Maybe she keeps her phone numbers nearby. What do you think?"

But Marie has stepped back down onto the lawn and looks around nervously. "I think we should leave. The neighbors might be watching."

"Chicken. Go sit in the car, then. I'm checking for a cell phone or work number for Brian." Annie opens the door wider and steps onto the threshold.

"I'm sure she knows her husband's number by heart. Come *on,* Annie."

"You go ahead. I'll be right with you. Won't touch a thing, I promise."

Marie scuttles off to the car as Annie steps inside.

She finds no list of numbers by the phone and looks around in the small kitchen. There's a fireplace, with logs neatly arranged to be lit. A few photographs rest on the mantelpiece. One is of Jean and a man Annie assumes to be Brian, taken when they were younger. Maybe it's a wedding photo. They are formally dressed, and Jean has a corsage pinned to her dress. Another photo shows the man alone. Quite a handsome fellow, Annie thinks. Suntanned, dark curly hair, a charming glint in his eye. How had the mousy Jean snagged a charmer like that?

There is one more picture on the mantel. It shows a big house on a tree-shaded street with a lake or river in the background. She looks closer at the photo. *Tulip trees,* she thinks. Tennessee's state tree. Also known as Yellow Poplar, which is something she knows because her reference librarian's brain is full of trivial and useless information like this. Next to the photos is a single yellow rose in a green glass vase; beside that, two pewter goblets. Annie had seen the goblets last week when Jean had just bought them from the Pewter Shop on Bearskin Neck. *"For a special occasion,"* Jean had said, before confessing with a blush that it was an anniversary. That same day—as in years past, Annie had remembered—a bouquet of yellow roses had been delivered to the main desk, with a card that read, "With all my love, Brian."

There are two place mats on the table, each with a folded paper napkin, a blue and white dinner plate, and nice silverware. *It sure looks as though Jean had been expecting Brian home for dinner last night. How odd that he hadn't showed up. Just when he was so desperately needed, too.* Annie looks over at the phone, which has an answering machine attached. The machine is blinking. One of the messages would be Duncan's call yesterday, trying to reach Brian. Annie is tempted to check the messages, but with her hand already raised above the handle, she hesitates and decides she'd better not. She looks around in the kitchen. There is a door next to the fireplace, and she opens it and walks into the living room, a large room with pale green walls and a bay window overlooking the garden.

"Anybody home? Brian, are you there?" she calls cautiously, but there is no answer.

The living room is lovely. The soft green is comforting, just the right shade to frame the view of Jean's flower garden in the summer. Yes, it is a lovely room—only, it stands empty, except for a couple of cardboard boxes. Annie lifts the flap of one.

Books. A scrapbook lies on top. She opens it and leafs through the first couple of pages, which are plastered with movie tickets, prom and concert programs, photos of Jean and her friends, and old newspaper clippings. A yellowed clipping from the *Louisville Gazette* shows Brian Stokes in uniform, captioned: "Louisville soldier headed for Grenada." Marie had remembered correctly, then. A bundle of yellowed letters, the bottom envelope addressed to Jean in neat fountain pen script—it had been sent out from Guam—all tied around with red ribbon, lie underneath the scrapbook. Old love letters, no doubt, from the years Brian was in the Navy.

"Annie, come *on,* let's go!" Marie has returned and calls from the doorstep. She is getting agitated, brushing the straight, gray bangs out of her eyes and pulling her raincoat tighter around her ample figure. The wind is picking up, and the sun has disappeared behind a cloud.

"I'll be right out!" Annie reluctantly drops the scrapbook and joins Marie outside, after twisting the knob on the handle to lock the kitchen door.

"No phone numbers," she reports. The rest she keeps to herself.

CHAPTER SEVEN

"How oft all men be cursed
By sharp-tongued wives.
Dost thou not wish to seek
A gentler maid?"
(Anon.)

"The room was empty, Dunc," Annie says. "What can it mean? Those boxes...it looks like someone's been packing to move. Do you think the Stokes could be splitting up... maybe he's leaving her, and that's what gave her a shock."

"Oh, Annie, please!" Duncan sounds exasperated.

"Please what? Somebody's got to do this, don't you see? Jean obviously doesn't have other family nearby, someone to look after her if anything happens to her. Let's call the hospital and find out how she is. I'll let you make the call. If I got that nurse from yesterday I'd probably be rude."

"Fine, I'll call. But don't stand next to me and kibbutz. Go on down to your desk. I'll buzz you as soon as I've talked to them. They must have gotten hold of Brian by now." *Please God,* he thinks.

Annie leaves to go back down to her desk, but not without putting on a sulky look. Duncan shakes his head, flashing her an unperturbed smile. He calls her on the intercom a few minutes later, sounding glum.

"They haven't located Brian yet. As a matter of fact, they were trying to pump *me* for information on how to contact him. I told them we didn't have his number."

"Did they tell you whether Brian is Jean's health care proxy?"

"Are you kidding? They're a close-lipped lot. They wouldn't even tell me whether Jean is awake yet."

"Or whether she's dead or alive?"

"No, not that either. We just have to be patient, my dear."

"Oh, are we back to 'my dear' again?"

"Only in the office."

"Okay then."

To get relief from her feeling of frustration, Annie impatiently rips into her paperwork pile. She has checked the number of sources available in the library on the current middle school project. Ample, if you include the archived *National Geographic* magazines and other science and nature materials that reside in the paper morgue downstairs in dusty stacks. An e-mail request for a biography of an early Rockport preacher sends her down to the local history room.

By coffee break she has put a good dent in the work, despite being interrupted by several phone requests. One of these, regarding an obscure and unfamiliar quote ascribed to Shakespeare, absorbs her for nearly an hour:

"How oft all men be cursed
By sharp-tongued wives.
Dost thou not wish to seek
A gentler maid?"

Annie's home library is largely devoted to Shakespeare—or "Willie," as she thinks of him affectionately. To her, he is nothing less than a dear and treasured friend who has seen her through some rough times. Her private bookshelves contain many old and valuable volumes of his works. Consequently, she is irritated—no, *incensed!*—at being stumped by a quote by the Bard. She checks the library's mammoth Shakespeare Concordance, then the convenient but less likely Bartlett's Quotations. When that does not yield a result, she tries a few of the major sources of quotations she has bookmarked on the Internet. In the end, looking at the quote again, she is disgusted with herself. Realizing that the quote is a fabrication, obviously pure invention by some wiseguy, she calls the patron with her verdict.

"Wow, not bad! Didn't think you'd be able to figure it out! Made it up myself."

Annie is in no mood for this kind of joke. She clenches her teeth.

"Very funny. Ha-ha. Well done." She tries to sound good-humored and cheery and hangs up carefully, fighting a strong urge to throw the phone across the room. Then she goes down to the dungeon. The librarians' cave-like lunchroom in the cellar lies in darkness. The old stone walls, as thick as in a castle keep, make for very deep windows, and these are placed high up on the wall, since most of the basement level lies underground. Only a faint light seeps in through the shrubbery, with the sun still on the other side of the building. She flips on the reading light over the round table and checks the coffee maker. The pot is half full of yesterday's cold coffee. She pours a mugful and zaps it in the microwave. Duncan would shudder; he is particular about his coffee.

Bringing her mug along, Annie walks out the back door and down into the library reading garden. The temperature must have reached a toasty fifty; it's comfortable outside even without a jacket. She puts the mug down on one of the benches and pulls out her cell phone. She can't very well make the long distance calls to Tennessee on the library phone, since they are not strictly reference calls—on top of which she is making the calls without asking for Duncan's go-ahead. Impatience and curiosity have gotten the better of her, as usual. The first telephone number on her list is no longer in service. She tries the next few and crosses them off before she gets to one listed to a Mitchell Stokes.

"That's me. Now, who ah you?"

"My name is Annie Quitnot. I'm calling from the Rockport Library. That's Rockport in Massachusetts, not in Maine. I'm actually looking for a *Brian* Stokes. Would he be a relative of yours?"

"Ah have a brothah by that name. Hwat do you want him for, Miss Quintott?"

"Eh, that's Quitnot, sir…I have a message for him. Do you think you could give me his number?"

"Well, now. Haven't spoke to him for a hwaahl. Brian left heah yeahs ago. Went into the sehvice. Moved to Virginny. Don't see much of him. He goes where the gov'mint sends him, ah guess. What's this all about then, Miss Quinton?"

"*Quit-not.* Ahem. Well, it's about his wife, actually, and it's an emergency. Do you have his number? This is a long distance…"

"His *hwaaf?* Now, what the heck kahnd of scam is this? Less'n she's risen from the dead, lahk Laz'rus! Miss *Quitnot,* eh? Is this supposed to be a joke, or hwat? Ah you maybe tryin' to git access to some o' his bank accounts? Well, ah'll be. Ah'll thank you nevah to call this numbah again."

"Oh, but…"

But Mr. Stokes has hung up. Annie shrugs. The wife is dead? Must be the wrong Brian Stokes. She sits for a while mulling over the phone call, left with an eerie feeling. After all, how many men named Brian Stokes could there be in Louisville, Tennessee, who had gone into the service? And now a new and entirely different idea has occurred to her, one that would be sure to drive Duncan up a wall, if she should spring it on him.

Instead, she calls Sally, her closest friend—someone she can always try her wild ideas out on. Sally and Annie think alike in many ways and enjoy solving the problems of the world, which they frequently do over a cup of tea or java at the local hangout.

"Hi Sal, want to meet me at the coffee shop in half an hour?"

"Just gotta blow-dry my hair, then I'll be there. What's up?"

"Wait 'til I see you. Just have to reduce the pile on my desk a bit first, or I'll get fired."

"Tcha, fat chance, you married to the boss. See you there."

CHAPTER EIGHT

"... and wicked dreams abuse
The curtain'd sleep..."
(Shakespeare, Macbeth)

Jean dreams.

Fighting with Mama, as usual. Mama says she can't go to the movies, even though all her friends are going, but Papa steps in, as he always does when he is home. Now she is getting ready, putting on her pretty plaid wool skirt, and brushing her hair. She has just washed her hair, and it's shiny. She's proud of her black hair and big violet eyes. Those are her pretty features. As for the rest...well, her face is too thin and her mouth too small—like a rosebud, Papa says. She smiles and puffs her cheeks out, which makes her look like a chipmunk. Then she lets the air out with a little sigh and dabs a dot of lipstick onto each cheek with her fingertips, rubbing it around vigorously. She squeezes her lips together hard to make them red. She doesn't want to use lipstick on her mouth, in case...just in case...Brian might try to kiss her. She will refuse, of course. Or will she? When the car honks in the driveway she runs out, grabbing her purse on the way and shouting "goodbye." She squeezes in next to Brian in the back seat, and the car roars off.

Jean smiles an inward smile, which would in any case remain unseen by Grace, the nurse on duty, who is focused on checking the drip. Grace squeezes the plastic bag a little. When she puts her hand around Jean's thin wrist to take her pulse, Jean's dream changes. It is Brian's hand she feels holding her wrist and looking into her eyes. Then Grace lets go, and so does Brian.

They have done a CT scan and the usual battery of tests on her. The fall had not caused any physical damage from what they could discover and had been ruled out as a cause for her state. Mrs. Stokes' brain seems to be alive and well. There is no evidence of an ischemic event, stroke or TIA, and no hemorrhage or sign of an aneurism is detected. Her heart is pumping gently and evenly. Her pulse races now and then, and Grace and the other nurses check it frequently. Grace shakes her head.

"Poor thing," she says. "Wake up." Then she becomes businesslike again and straightens the bedding, which, since Jean hasn't moved, is already impeccable. Before she leaves, she pulls the curtain across a little, to shield the patient from the bright light.

Don't leave me, Jean thinks. *Brian, come back.* Her dream turns dark again, and she sinks deeper into a black and disturbing state of unconsciousness._

CHAPTER NINE

"Holla your name to the reverberate hills,
And make the babbling gossip of the air..."
(Shakespeare, Twelfth Night)

To make sure they get a good seat, Sally has hurried to take one of the small side tables in the coffee shop, and has ordered her usual, tea and Nisu. She sips the tea, twisting a short, dark curl around her finger. Sally, who is a year older than Annie, looks and dresses like a teenager and can still get away with it. She works in one of the gift shops on Bearskin Neck in the summer, but during the school year she stays home, having her hands full with her twin teenage boys. While waiting for Annie, she looks around. The coffee shop has just changed hands. Still in the same family, it's now run by grandsons of Phyllis' and Archie's, and renamed Brothers Brew. The missing counter stools have been replaced, and a cheery paint job brightens the place, turning it into something like a comfortable diner with a Provence café attitude. Some new goodies sit displayed on glass cake stands along the back wall. *That seven layer bar will have to be tested,* Sally thinks. The most important fact, however, is that the baker still produces the famous Nisu, the braided Finnish coffee bread, to the relief of the regulars.

Lunchtime is busy time, and Sally and Annie never want to end up at the counter, where even a whisper can be picked up by a neighbor. When Annie arrives, she gets her coffee mug filled and brings it over to the side table.

"So, what's new?" Sally bites into her piece of toasted Nisu, which they always order with the works—buttered and dredged in sugar and cinnamon.

"Well, I don't know whether you've heard about Jean?"

"I heard. How's she doing?"

"We don't know. The hospital won't give us any information. As far as we know, they haven't been able to locate her husband. So there she lies, in limbo. I don't know how they are even able to make a decision about what to do for her. What if it's a life threatening situation?"

Sally shakes her head and takes another bite. Annie, who is hungry, has ordered a spicy Boom Boom Chicken on Ciabatta. The sandwich comes with a bag of chips, which she struggles to open. Finally she succeeds above expectation, the chips shooting out over the table and onto the floor. She picks one off the floor and pops it into her mouth.

"Yeech." Sally wrinkles her nose.

"Felix!"

"Oscar!"

"Come on, I followed the five-second-rule."

The counter seats are filled, and the next customers have to squeeze in to stand in the take-out area just inside the door, by a little table with napkins and condiments. The usual din erupts while the daily gossip is aired. Annie and Sally take the time to down a few bites while they listen in.

"Did you hear about the middle school fracas the other night?" Billy Eakins, one of the school janitors, who is sitting at the last counter seat, asks his neighbor.

"You mean at hockey practice? Yeah."

"What happened?" someone who hasn't heard yet butts in.

"Well, Jack Davis had it out with Larry Petersen. Said his son Tim wasn't getting enough ice time. Then, when Tim used his stick on a kid and Coach Petersen threw him out, Davis went after the coach."

"Knocked him out, from what I heard."

"Drunk, probably. Jack's a mean drunk," someone at the other end of the counter offers.

"He's been barred from the rink for the rest of the school year."

"Coach should sue him," someone mumbles.

"Petersen's a'ready talked to a lahyah." Joe Brackett, a local oldtimer, joins the conversation. "He tole me Davis is abaht to get suhved—today, prob'ly. Meanwhile, Larry's on sick leave until aftah Thanksgivin'. Left yestaday fah his cabin down Maine. Said he means to do some fishin'—and wait for the bruises to fade, I don' doubt. Looked like his nose was broke." Brackett, whose leathery skin is a result of many hours at sea, sometimes takes Larry out fishing in his lobster boat. "He fayvahs the lakes up theah, you know. Larry's a landlubbah, don' handle ocean swells too good," he adds with a chuckle. "I'm goin' up theah this weekend to do some lake fishin' with 'im. Don' much care fah those yella' lake fish, but what the heck. Larry's a nahs guy. We'll have a cupla beahs an' grill the fish good 'n black on the camp fyiah so's you don' know the diff'rence anyhow."

Sally has stopped chewing. Jack and Lorraine Davis are her neighbors, and she is, inexplicably, a good friend of Lorraine's. To Annie, Lorraine is simply an intolerable pest, always demanding special privileges for her son Tim at the library. Tim, who is a classmate of Sally's twins, Ben and Brad, is the apple of his mother's eye and can do no wrong. Sally's son Brad is also on the hockey team, and Annie wonders why Sally hasn't told her about the "fracas." But Sally is a forgiving sort and has a soft spot for Lorraine that defies explanation. Sally looks at Annie with a bleak smile and a half guilty shrug.

"Brad told me about it. Awful, isn't it? Poor Lorraine," she says, and that's the end of that conversation.

Annie still remembers how Lorraine had tried to get the library to fire Sally's son Ben for getting his lip pierced and hire her son Tim as a page instead. *Tim would benefit so much more from it—after all, he's on track to go to college,* she had told Duncan. Sally had just smiled that understanding-mother-smile when Annie told her. Now Annie doesn't even want to mention the fact that Lorraine has just volunteered to decorate the library Christmas tree, something she had originally planned to gripe about. Anyway, Sally would only consider that as proof of what a nice person Lorraine really is. They've been through this many times, each time agreeing to differ when it comes to Lorraine.

"And how is that librarian of yours?" Mrs. Sweeney, who works for the Smythe Agency, one of the local real estate agents, swirls around on her stool and looks questioningly at Annie. "Mrs. Stokes, I mean. Spoke to that Mrs. Ridley (Mrs. Ridley is frequently referred to as *that* Mrs. Ridley), and she said old Mr. Hale had told her he'd seen a moving van coming down from that direction. Are the Stokes moving? That's a nice prop'ty. Are they selling, you think? How is she, anyway? Better, I hope."

"They won't tell us, since they've been unable to reach her husband so far," Annie says, staying away from the rest of the questions.

Some people just can't pass up an opportunity to make a buck. Frederick Smythe, Mrs. Sweeney's boss, is known for having a nose for lucrative deals, and Mrs. Sweeney would receive a decent finder's fee if she were to scoop the Stokes' property. Seeing she is not going to get anything out of Annie, Mrs. Sweeney turns away. The counter crowd loses interest and starts discussing the condition of the roads, and then go on to politics and the usual town gossip, and Annie and Sally tune them out.

"So what was it you wanted to talk to me about?" Sally asks.

"Too many people in here; let's take a quick walk."

"It's cold out there, and windy. Practically winter."

"Sissy. Anyway, it's almost fifty, practically spring."

"Well, all right, then. This better be good, Annie." Sally swigs her tea as fast as she can.

They walk down Main Street toward Bearskin Neck. The wind has come back, and whips around between the buildings, bringing gusts of salt-saturated air and a gentle smell of rotting seaweed.

"It's about Jean. You can't talk to anyone about this, Sal. Marie and I went up to her house this morning to see if Brian was back yet. Well, he still hadn't come home. According to Marie, Brian's job takes him away a lot. Anyway, the back door was unlocked, so I went in."

She goes on to describe what she had found.

"So, Mrs. Sweeney may be right, then? About them moving?" Sally says.

Annie frowns before shrugging and shaking her head. "Oh, I don't think so, Sal. Not both of them, anyway. After seeing that empty room, all I could think was that Brian had left her. It would have given her such a shock, Sally, especially right after their anniversary. You know how sensitive she is. What occurred to me was that if he had just left her, Jean might have panicked and OD'd on something, like sleeping pills or tranquilizers... but I'm sure they would have caught that at the hospital."

"What, taken and overdose and then gone to work? That doesn't sound rational."

"Well, people don't always act rationally..."

"You should ask, I guess." Sally doesn't sound convinced.

"Yes, well, I suppose. But Sally, say that Brian really did leave...why would he bother to take the furniture, but then leave her with the house? I just can't figure this out. There wasn't a thing left in the living room. No pictures on the walls, no curtains, no rugs. Wasn't any of it hers? I wish I'd taken that scrapbook of hers along. There might be some information in it that would help us locate Brian. Anyway, it was kind of eerie, seeing that empty room. The kitchen is still all furnished, right down to the logs in the fireplace and the table set for two. What seems strange to me is that everything obviously appeared fine to Jean last week. She was so excited planning for their anniversary, and then he sent flowers to her at the library, and she said they'd had a lovely dinner. So, why didn't he come back the other night? She was obviously expecting him. Or...maybe he *did* come back..." Annie suddenly has another thought.

The wind is ripping at their clothes, and Sally pulls her crocheted wool hat down over her ears, complaining loudly. Annie is merciless. She strides on, with Sally jogging behind. They are halfway down Bearskin Neck by now, and Annie isn't slowing down. Many of the galleries and quaint shops are boarded up for the winter. Even the Strudel Shop is closed up tight, the big sail shading the verandah put away until next year. Strudels will be available only on fair-weather weekends during the winter season. A few shop owners stick it out until after Christmas, and a small number of true diehards brave the winter and stay open year round. Many of the artists disappear for points south: Florida, the Southwest, Mexico, or some island off Greece or Italy. Sally moans pitifully as they near the end of the Neck, where there are no houses or shacks to give protection from the whistling wind and the foam that's being thrown into the air by the waves. Big swells are breaking over the jetty, and the boulders rumble dully as they roll back and forth.

"Do we have to go any further? I don't feel like going for a swim," Sally shouts.

Annie shakes her head at this sort of weakness and continues, in a voice loud enough to overpower the waves, by telling Sally about the phone call to Mitchell Stokes. When she comes to the part about the dead wife, Sally's eyes go wide. They have stalled long enough out at the end of the neck, and Annie finally relents and turns around. After a short jog, the wind now mercifully at their back, they reach the safety of small shacks and cottages again. They stop and take the scant shelter offered by the doorway of the Country Store, where Annie waits to let Sally's brainwaves catch up with her own. Finally, the light dawns.

"You think Brian tried to kill her? "

"Well, what else? Anyway, that's the possibility that just occurred to me. Maybe he was having an affair—you know, being away so much, maybe he gets lonely. He's a handsome guy, from the photos I saw of him in the kitchen. Looks like he might be a bit of a rogue. What if he, you know, laced Jean's coffee or something? I know, I know, you think my imagination is running away with me, but I'm beginning to feel that there is something very odd going on here. I mean, why else hasn't he come home by now? Wouldn't he have called to tell her if his plans had changed? Wouldn't he be concerned if he couldn't reach her on the phone? I mean, don't married people call each other to chat about their day when they are apart? Wouldn't he have tried to reach her at the library if he couldn't get hold of her at home?"

"You're right. There's something funny about that."

"After all, we don't know for sure whether he was home the morning she collapsed in the library or not, but we do know that he was there for their anniversary just a few nights earlier, because she told us about it the day after. Now, Sal, imagine it this way: If he does work for the FBI, he'll probably have access to some hard-to-detect poisoning agents. What if he left her a poisoned something, like a chocolate truffle, to go with her morning coffee? *'Oh, what a sweet thing to do, he's left me a treat,'* she'd say. She'd take a bite, close her eyes while the chocolate melted in her mouth. Can't you see her? We all know Jean's weakness for truffles. That's what the librarians get her for her birthday every year, a box of truffles from Tuck's. Brian could have left town the night before, even, and been far away when she found the little treat in the morning. He might be in Hawaii by now, for all we know."

"So, how come she didn't die at home, alone?"

"Maybe she brought it to work with her..."

"So, then, without waiting around to make sure she was dead, he would have called his brother to give him the sad news?" Sally says, looking doubtful.

"Hm. I don't know. But why else would Mitchell say that Brian's wife was dead? I'm still not clear about why Brian would have called to tell him; it didn't sound to me as though they were close. But maybe it was part of some elaborate alibi Brian was trying to create? You know, letting someone know that he was far away from home when she died. Calling from a hotel that the call could be traced back to."

"But, Annie, if Brian was far away when she...well, when he *assumed* she died, how would he explain *finding out* about her death?"

"I'm sure he has that covered." Annie sounds somewhat less confident now.

"But wouldn't the sad news make him rush back home? You know, to arrange the funeral, for instance?"

"No idea. You ask too many questions, Sal, and I've got to get back to work. I'll call you later."

"If there's any more walking and talking involved, let's do it indoors. Meet and walk at the mall, or something."

"Weak as water, that's what you are."

CHAPTER TEN

"Silence is the perfectest herald of joy:
I were but little happy, if I could say how much."
(Shakespeare, Much Ado About Nothing)

Jean dreams.

It is a special evening, and she and Brian are driving into Knoxville for dinner. Dusk is falling, the countryside flies by in the last gleams of the sun. The golden ribbon of the Tennessee River appears now and then between the trees. The river meanders, sometimes widening until it looks like a lake. They are traveling along the Alcoa Highway, nearing the city. She can see the lights already, and remembers the excitement she had felt when she was a little girl and her parents had taken her into Knoxville. The river, over on their left, makes one of its many sinuous bends. The sun has set, and the water lies in shadow, the color of lead. The Looney Islands are barely visible in the dark. They cross the river and take West Cumberland into downtown. She braids her fingers together, anxious and eager at the same time, hoping this is the night Brian will ask her the big question.

They pull into a well-lit parking lot, and Brian helps her out of the car. Before tossing his overcoat into the trunk, he pulls a transparent plastic container from the coat pocket. He opens it and pulls out a corsage, a white orchid with pinkish edges and little pink dots in the center. He tries to pin it to her dress, but she has to help him. Her fingers tremble slightly when they touch his.

The restaurant is not far. Brian has reserved a table. White linen tablecloth, linen napkins. A yellow rose in a tall, narrow vase. He must have ordered it special; the other tables all have carnations.

Brian opens the menu.

"Let me order. You'll just pick the cheapest thing...I know you."

They have red wine with the steak, which is tender and very salty. Mama never uses enough salt in her cooking. The table is cleared, and Brian orders dessert. Crème Brulé for her; he knows it's her favorite.

While they wait, he fusses a little while getting something out of his jacket pocket and hides it under the napkin. He reaches across the table and takes her hand. Right there in the restaurant, in front of all those strangers, Brian takes her hand.

"Jean, will you marry me?"

It is suddenly quiet in the restaurant, and Brian's voice seems so loud to her—reverberating in the room and bouncing around in her head. The violinist, who had been walking around from table to table earlier, must be off in another area of the restaurant. She can only nod; her breath catches in her chest, almost making her cough. Brian pulls a little box out from under the napkin. He opens it himself and slips the ring on her finger. The small diamond glitters brightly in the candlelight when she twists her hand. People at nearby tables have turned to look at them. An elderly man raises his glass to toast them, winking. Someone starts applauding, and others join in. She manages a smile, a tense, trembling smile, and blushes. Why does she always have to blush? Now the violinist returns, probably prompted by one of the guests, and asks what they would like to hear. Brian whispers in his ear. The violinist plays "The Tennessee Waltz," and Brian gets up and takes her by the hand. He leads her to the dance floor, where they are soon joined by other couples.

The Crème Brulé has arrived when they sit back down, but she is too excited to touch it. Brian is talking about their honeymoon. Where would she like to go? Her head is swimming; she has no idea.

"Hawaii?"

No, too far. "I've always wanted to see New England," she says, "you know, one of those quaint little fishing villages."

Brian laughs.

"Then New England it is. Cape Ann, isn't that where they do a lot of fishing?"

She smiles. It doesn't matter much to her where they go. Brian takes her hand again and looks into her eyes. She has often wondered, when she's been at the movies, how that would feel. To have Cary Grant or some other handsome man looking deep into your eyes. Now she knows. The elderly man has been watching them, and now he gets up and comes over to their table.

"Would you like me to take a picture of the two of you? This is a moment to remember, after all."

Brian looks at her, and she nods, feeling the blush creep into her cheeks again. The man takes a couple of shots, and Jean jots down her address on the back of an envelope and gives it to him.

Grace thinks her patient looks flushed, but there are no other signs that would give cause for worry. She hurriedly goes through the usual routine before rushing off to tend to the several new patients in the ward, some of them requiring more urgent care than the quiet Mrs. Stokes does.

CHAPTER ELEVEN

"Slander,
Whose edge is sharper than the sword,
Whose tongue outvenoms all the worms of Nile. . ."
(Shakespeare, Cymbeline)

On the way back to work, Annie stops at Town Hall. She goes into the assessor's office, where she finds that the Stokes' house on Old Quarry Lane is listed in Jean's name only. *Aha.* That could explain why Brian only took his furniture and left Jean with the house. She owns it. The arrangement is not that unusual. Some people do that. *In fact,* Annie thinks suddenly, *my house is in my name, and Duncan's is in his. Hm. Suppose something will have to be done about that eventually.* When she checks on car registrations, resident parking, recycling and dump stickers, only Jean's name appears. But then, Brian may be driving a government car registered somewhere else.

Back at the library she goes into her file drawer and pulls out the Street Listing, generally called the *nosey book*, which lists the town's residents. Brian is not in it, only Jean. Not much other information to be gleaned there, except that Jean is a registered voter, a library assistant, and is forty-two years old. Annie is shocked at this last piece of information. She would have guessed Jean to be at least fifty. Jean's hair, while still black, has fine, gray strands in it. Her face is thin and not particularly lined, but there are often dark shadows under those big, violet eyes of hers, giving her a look of being an older woman. But why isn't Brian listed in the nosey book? Must be his job. People in sensitive positions are often left out of the street listing. Or perhaps Brian prefers to be registered to vote somewhere else, maybe at his other residence, where he apparently spends most of his time.

Marie beckons for Annie to come to the main desk. Duncan has hired Penny to sub for Jean, but Penny is out to lunch, and Marie needs to help a patron find a book. Annie takes over at the desk. When Marie comes back, she sighs.

"Oh, Annie, I miss Jean. Nothing is functioning properly today. Penny is a nice person, but you have to tell her how to do everything. She doesn't remember a thing from one day to the next, even how to do a simple renewal. *Oh, is this the right screen, Marie? Am I doing this right, Marie? Do I hit enter now?*"

Annie nods in sympathy.

"Do you want me to stay here until Penny gets back? Why don't you go and get a cup of coffee or something."

"No, no. You've got your own load. Any news on Jean?"

"Not that I've heard. I haven't checked with Duncan since before lunch."

"Uh-oh, I think you've got a customer. Run along."

Marie gives Annie a funny look, which Annie understands when she looks up and the "customer" (as they are *not* supposed to refer to their patrons) turns out to be Mrs. Ridley. Annie walks to the reference desk and takes her seat.

"Well, *Mizzz.* Quitnot," This is the way Mrs. Ridley addresses Annie, who has decided to keep her maiden name after marriage. "what's the news on our poor librarian?"

"I'm sorry, Mrs. Ridley, we don't know. Until the hospital reaches her husband, they will not give out any information."

"Out of town, is he? A rare bird, that one. Well, I heard from Johnnie Hale, who lives next door to me, that the Stokes' house is being emptied out. Said he saw a moving van on the street recently. I went over to check, being neighborly. Now that nobody's at home there, us neighbors will have to keep a lookout. Their living room's empty, that much I could see. Looks to me like somebody's moving out. So, right away people think it's him leaving her. Why would a man leave his house and just take some of the furniture, I ask you? Makes no sense to me. What, then? Maybe *she's* the one that's moving out, I say. And, maybe Mr. Stokes isn't out of town after all. Maybe the police ought to check the basement. Well, why not? Things like that are in the papers every day. She could sell that house for a mint, mind you me. It would be an easy thing for her to start a rumor that they're moving and suggest that Mr. Stokes has gone ahead somewhere. Mrs. Stokes may look like a delicate thing, but I've seen her working around the yard, digging and hoeing and pushing her wheelbarrow around. I wouldn't put it past her, doing him in. But then, after the deed, maybe the stress became too much for her, and that's what put her in the hospital."

Annie, who has been listening in mute astonishment, finally gets her tongue back.

"Mrs. Ridley, that's a terrible accusation. You should be careful to not spread that kind of speculation." Annie pulls out a file from her drawer and bends over it. "I'm sorry, Mrs. Ridley, but I have a lot of work to do right now."

"Well, if that's how you feel. We'll see who's right. I'm going over to speak to Chief Murphy right now. In fact, I consider it my civic duty."

Annie watches Mrs. Ridley's offended, ramrod back as the woman leaves the reference department. As soon as this detestable "customer" goes out the door, Annie buzzes Duncan on the intercom.

"Duncan, we've got a problem."

CHAPTER TWELVE

". . . welcome ever smiles,
And farewell goes out sighing."
(Shakespeare, Troilus and Cressida)

Jean dreams.

Brian will be home any time now. She goes outside and picks the last two yellow roses on the bush by the doorway. The rest of the garden has gone by. She sticks them into her favorite vase, the green glass one that Brian gave her for her birthday once. Then she sets the table, after first removing the plastic tablecloth she uses when she eats alone. She replaces it with a nice white linen square, with her initials, JS, embroidered in the corner. Her mother always set great store by her own linen, especially the damask. She gets two napkins to match, freshly ironed, out of the drawer and folds them into a crisp triangle, making sure the initials are showing on top. She puts the vase in the center of the table, a candle on each side. Brian's favorite dish is in the oven: beef stew made with carrots and onions. She whips the mashed potato and puts it in a covered bowl, with a sprig of parsley for garnish. She has made the cranberry relish herself, with berries she picked in Dogtown just after they were nipped with frost, when they develop their best taste. She checks her watch and takes off her apron when she hears the sound of a car. Oh, the candles. Mustn't forget to light the candles. Then she hurries to open the door to welcome him.

She dishes out potatoes for him, chooses the best pieces of meat, and puts them neatly on the plate with a few carrots.

"Would you like some extra gravy, honey? Here, help yourself to some of my cranberry sauce." She serves herself and sits down. She lifts her glass, a goblet with an etched flower design, in a toast.

"Welcome home. Oh, Brian, you don't know how awfully I miss you when you're gone!"

Grace stands over her patient, checking her pulse. It's fast again. She rechecks it before writing it down. It's dark outside now, and she turns on the small light in back of the bed. Jean seems oblivious to the change. Tiny beads of sweat glisten along the hairline, and Grace mops them off. *Someone in her family should sit here and talk to her,* she thinks, but Grace has other patients to tend to and must run along. When she comes back, later in the evening, there is a guard posted outside Jean's door. Grace is allowed in to perform her duties, with the guard standing in the doorway.

"Why does she have to have a guard?" Grace asks as she is leaving.

"Couldn't tell ya," he says.

Couldn't or wouldn't? she wonders.

Jean stirs in her bed, twisting her head.

Brian is gone again.

CHAPTER THIRTEEN

"There's nothing ill can dwell in such a temple..."
(Shakespeare, The Tempest)

Bella the Singer is walking through the library. It's only a matter of time before all hell breaks loose. Annie looks around to see who else is in the library. Most of the regular patrons put up with Bella, but outsiders sometimes get uncomfortable. Bella is quite a sight. As long as she keeps quiet, though, everything will be fine. *But, oh no, there she goes.*

"Napaleeeeete, magaleeeeete,
Nooka, nooka, mooora loo,
Camari-na, polasi-na,
Ca-me, ca-me, reema-do."

Bella's high-pitched singing is enough to alarm most people, even those who are used to her, and strangers in the library are already running for the nearest exit, sure that something untoward is about to happen. Annie gets up from her desk.

"Bella, dear," she says, walking up to the singer, who is meandering between the stacks. Bella's attire is an interesting mix: a black, tattered men's suit and a white shawl with large, red flowers. The outfit is topped off with a bowler, tilted slightly, as if ready for a sweeping Broadway gesture. She carries her belongings in a large nylon bag that exudes a mildly distressing odor. Annie knows better than to touch her, even gently. Bella does not like to be touched. That would set off a tirade, sometimes even produce a flurry of violent kicking and shoving, and Annie is intent on getting Bella out of the library before Stuart hears her.

"It's such a lovely day outside, Bella. Why don't you go on down to Millbrook Meadow? The birds will be so happy to see you. You know how they like to sing along with you," she says, guiding Bella with gestures toward the door.

Bella does not speak. No one seems to know whether this is because she has forgotten how or because she never knew how. Some of the meaner people in town say that Bella is only pretending, so that she can live on the dole, but Annie feels that there is a lost soul inside that lovely carapace. She may appear an empty building, but somewhere in there, the soul is alive and stirring. Bella, who probably is in her late thirties, has long, blond hair, which is as unkempt as her clothing. Her facial features are stunning, if anyone were to take a good look, but she is usually so grimy and odiferous that people prefer to turn away.

Whatever happened to you to make you this way? Annie wonders, for the thousandth time.

Bella follows Annie toward the exit and gives her a ravishing smile as she walks out the door.

"Raheee-ma, maseee-ma,
Da-lee, da-lee, raama,
Gali, gali, nerema."

Bella continues singing at the top of her voice while she walks down the front steps and points her nose in the direction of the meadow.

Annie sighs. *Far too much sighing going on lately,* she thinks.

Stuart comes skipping down the stairs, hands in pockets, looking around eagerly. Stuart loves a spot of trouble. "Did I hear Bella again?"

"She's on her way to the meadow, I believe," Annie says casually.

"People like that should be barred from the library."

"It's a public place, Stuart, and she's not harming anyone." Annie is beginning to sound less casual.

"They should never have closed all those places and let those people out. They're a menace to society and themselves."

"There but for the grace of God…" Annie says, feeling morally superior and smug about subjecting Stuart to some of his own treatment. She smiles blithely and turns on her heel, and then she thinks of Jean and hopes fervently that another mind is not in the process of being emptied.

As soon as Stuart disappears back upstairs, Esa Kauppila, the janitor, comes out of his place of hiding in the stacks. Whenever Bella shows up, Esa finds an out-of-the-way spot to do his sweeping and dusting. Esa is a cheerful sort, actually a man in his forties, although they all think of him as a boy. A somewhat limited mental capacity has left him at the level of a young teenager. Esa is smart in many ways and frequently makes unexpectedly lucid assessments of people. He is wary of Stuart, knowing how the children's librarian feels about people like him.

"Mr. Swell is mean to Bella. She means no harm. She looks so happy when she sings, Miss Annie." Esa has difficulties with names. Stuart Cogswell becomes "Mr. Swell," Duncan Langmuir is "Mr. Lammer," and the women are "Miss Annie, Miss Marie, Miss Maureen, Miss Clare, and Miss Jean."

"I know, Esa. I only told her to leave so Mr. Cogswell wouldn't catch her and say something mean to her. You know how she is when she gets upset."

"Yes, I do. She told me she hates him."

Annie is astonished. "You mean she *talks* to you?"

"Of course, Miss Annie. Sometimes we walk together, and I share my sangwich with her if she doesn't have anythin' to eat.

She gets real hungry, and she looks in the trash barrels for food, and I tell her not to 'cause it'll make her sick."

Annie would like to hear more about Bella and regrets that duty is calling.

"Sorry, Esa, have to run. I have an errand to Town Hall. It's my turn to pick up the checks, you see. I'm late already, and some people around here get a little aggravated if they don't get their money into the bank on payday."

"Oh, it's okay, Miss Annie. I wouldn't never get aggarvated at you. I know you have a lot to do. I'll take care of the plants on top of your virgical file while you're gone. When the sun shines on the leaves you can see how dusty they are."

"Thank you, Esa; you are so thoughtful. I appreciate the way you take care of my reference area." She has to steel herself not to giggle at his reference to the vertical file, which takes up the entire length of the wall behind her.

CHAPTER FOURTEEN

*"It takes little talent to see clearly what lies under one's nose,
A good deal of it to know in which direction to point that organ"
(W. H. Auden, The Dyer's Hand)*

"We've got to call Judge." Annie takes the pot off the burner and stirs vigorously. Chowder should never be allowed to boil, lest it turn bitter. She adds a little cream to sweeten it, just in case.

"Good idea!" Duncan hopes that Judge Bradley can bring some sanity to the situation. Things are starting to get out of hand. Another scandal seems to be looming over the library.

The salad is ready, and Annie sprinkles some Parmesan cheese on the toasted and buttered dill bread. It's her day to cook and Duncan's turn to set the table.

"Let's eat in the rough," Annie says, and Duncan nods happily. He picks a pair of brown crockery mugs and sets out a roll of paper towels instead of napkins.

When Annie told Duncan earlier what Mrs. Ridley had suggested, he had been just as shocked and dumbfounded as she. As expected, Mrs. Ridley had made good on her threat to go to the police station. Chief Murphy had listened, with what degree of disbelief they could only imagine. Chief Murphy is a master of disbelief, but he also knows that he has to act on an accusation, whether he likes it or not. The chief had decided that if there was even a possibility that Mrs. Ridley's outrageous ramblings could turn out to be true, he would have to leave a guard outside Mrs. Stokes' hospital room. Then he had sent Officer Hale to have a look at the Stokes' home. Billy Hale had returned and reported that parts of the house, from what he could see through the windows, were indeed empty, and that there were no cars in the garage. He had also mentioned Ms. Quitnot's request that Mrs. Stokes' car, which was parked in the library lot, would not get any overnight parking tickets while the woman was in the hospital. The chief had cast a weary eye at his watch while Officer Hale rattled on.

"I don't suppose you checked the doors?"

"Front and back doors were locked."

Chief Murphy had pondered Billy's observations for a while. Then he had taken the cruiser and gone up to Old Quarry Lane, search warrant secure in his pocket, to see for himself, taking Officer Hale along. The chief had raised one of the garage doors and found the door leading from there into the house unlocked. The first thing they had done was to go down and check the basement for a dead body or signs of digging. The basement had a solid cement floor that looked as old as the house. It would take a jackhammer to dig a grave down there.

"Well, that takes care of that," the chief had mumbled, sounding satisfied.

Back upstairs, they had wandered through the house. The kitchen had looked perfectly normal. Neat as a pin, as he had expected. Mrs. Stokes always appeared neat and proper. The chief had noted that the table was set for two, and that would have been on the day of Mrs. Stokes' collapse in the library. But Mr. Stokes, which the chief found a little odd under the circumstances, had not turned up. Looking around, Chief Murphy had noted that the kitchen fireplace mantel held a couple of photographs, one of the Stokes couple, the chief assumed, with Mrs. Stokes looking younger and quite pretty. It looked to have been taken in a restaurant. The other one was an old black and white of a house. Next to the photographs there had been a vase with a wilted flower and a couple of goblets.

They had continued through the house. Mrs. Ridley had been right: the living room was empty, except for a couple of cardboard boxes that looked to be filled with books and papers. There were two bedrooms in the house, one empty and one sparsely furnished with a narrow bed, a small bureau, and white curtains. The bureau held another photograph of a young Mr. and Mrs. Stokes, walking in a field with a lake or river in the background, arms around each other, smiling and squinting into the sun.

The bed had been neatly made. There was one small rug in the room, right next to the bed. *Just big enough to plant your feet on when you got out of bed on a cold morning,* the chief had thought. The closet door had stood open, and the chief had noted that it only held dresses and other women's clothing. There had been no sign of Mr. Stokes' clothes or personal belongings in the other bedroom or anywhere else in the house. In the end, the kitchen had been the only place that looked normal.

They had left the same way they came, and the chief, looking thoughtful, had pulled down the garage door before they returned to the station. The state of Jean Stokes' house had certainly raised questions in his mind. Could there be something to what that obnoxious woman had said after all?

• • •

Annie calls Judge and Josie, and Judge picks up.

"Hi, Judge, I'm calling about Jean Stokes—you know, one of my colleagues. She's been taken to the hospital, and we can't find out how she's doing. We're getting really worried." Annie tells Judge everything except her own speculations. She will wait to hear what he infers from the bare facts. Well, as bare as she can manage. Judge will scramble them all in his clever brain, and some valuable revelation is sure to result.

"Let me look into it, m'dear. I'll call the chief and milk whatever I can out of him. Then I'll check with the hospital. Sounds like your Mrs. Stokes is going to need an advocate to speak for her. Maybe I'll volunteer my services until she recovers consciousness."

"Thanks a mil; that sounds like just the ticket. Now, can I talk to Josie? I'd like to plan a get-together before the holidays start piling up."

"She's right here, trying to wrest the phone away from me. You girls set it up. I'll call you when I have something to report."

Annie and Josie make plans for a casual evening at Judge's place later in the week. It will be the usual potluck affair, with Josie doing the main dish, Annie tossing one of her surprise salads, and Duncan plotting some fabulous dessert. Judge will open his liquor cabinet, and an appropriate bottle of wine will be either chilled or simply uncorked and left to breathe for the required time.

Judge Bradley has been a judge so long that no one remembers his actual first name, and in consequence everyone calls him "Judge," as though it were his christened name. Judge has the stature and demeanor, not to mention those steely, blue eyes, to encourage bits of information out of most people, including the chief of police and assorted town officials, despite the fact that he has been retired for years. This is what Annie is counting on now, in order to help Jean. And to solve what is turning into an odd mystery.

Sitting down with Duncan again, Annie sighs.

"You're sighing a lot lately, darling."

"Oh, I'm so glad we're back to *darling.* Anyway, I assure you, *that* one was definitely a sigh of relief, now that Judge is aboard. How about let's put all this aside and spend the evening on something totally different?" she says, taking a sip of Duncan's freshly brewed coffee.

"Well, now. I might have a few ideas. Very brilliant ones, if I say so myself."

CHAPTER FIFTEEN

"Sleep, sleep: in thy sleep
Little sorrows sit and weep"
(William Blake, "A Cradle Song,")

Jean's head turns almost imperceptibly toward the light. *"Wait 'til you hear this, Brian! I applied for a job at the library, and I've been accepted! I didn't tell you, but I had an interview with the trustees last week. I didn't think it went very well; you know how tongue-tied I get when I'm nervous. That's why I didn't tell you. But I got the job!"*

She chatters away while clearing the table and rinsing the dishes carefully before stacking them in the dishwasher. Afterwards she pulls some papers out of a manila envelope and sits back down at the table. The tip of her tongue sticks out between her lips while she concentrates on filling out the town employee form that has to be filed before she can start.

"Oh, there's a section here on the husband's employment...what shall I fill in? It's not really any of their business anyway, is it? I'll just leave it blank. Wouldn't that be best? If they ask me, I'll say 'it's classified.' It won't be a lie. Everything's classified, right? People, flowers, animals...right? Okay, that's what I'm doing."

She signs her name neatly on the last page and puts the form back in the envelope. She will turn it in tomorrow, and next week she will be a regular library employee! Oh, if Papa could see her now! Mama, too, for that matter. Mama never thought she would amount to anything. Well, Mama was wrong.

Grace studies the peaceful face of her patient. Normal blood pressure. Everything about Mrs. Stokes seems normal today, except that the woman is in a coma and appears to be making no progress. Grace leaves the room, heading for her other duties, and Jean enters another dream.

"Well, Brian, Mrs. Davis—you know that woman who always tries to get away with things in the library—she was in again today. I hoped Marie would be the one to check her books out. Mrs. Davis always gets me in trouble. Maybe if I get busy at the trolley, I thought. But, oh-no, too late, she caught my eye, kept me in her sight, and marched right up."

Jean squirms, but no one is there to notice. The room is gloomy, the sun has gone behind a cloud, but it makes no difference to Jean anymore. She is in another country, in a time no longer of her own choosing. Images appear; she cannot close them out. All she can do is squirm in discomfort.

"Mrs. Davis plunked her stack of books down next to my computer. Sure enough, she was trying to get away with taking more than allowed for that little darling Timmy of hers. And, as usual, she got her way. I'm no match for her. She left, smirking at me, knowing she'd had me again. People are always taking advantage of me, just like you told me, Brian. I used to think my way was the right way: treat everyone kindly, kindness is its own reward, but I don't get rewarded. I just get in trouble for it."

Suddenly, the sun strikes her face. A narrow beam has discovered the window and is making a brief visit before it hits the window frame. It warms her for a few minutes, then slides off and seeks a new target. But it lasts long enough to end one dream and begin another.

She hears the knock on the door, but hides, pretending not to be home. The knock is repeated, louder. She peeks through the thin curtains. Mrs. Ridley stands outside with a napkin-covered plate, and Mrs. Ridley will know she is at home because her car is parked right outside. Nothing for it but to open the door. Who knows what the woman might think if she didn't. Maybe that she was entertaining a gentleman or some such outrageous thing.

"Yes, Mrs. Ridley, what can I do for you?"

"Oh, nothing, dear, it's the other way around. I'm just being neighborly. Thought I might catch you at tea time. Maybe you'd like a slice of my lemon tea bread to go with it?"

Of course, now the woman expects to be asked in.

"Why, thank you, Mrs. Ridley. Unfortunately, I was just getting ready to go out. I have an appointment." She reaches out to accept the plate, but Mrs. Ridley has quickly withdrawn it, now that she's not invited in. "Sorry, Mrs. Ridley, another time, maybe," she says a little lamely.

Embarrassed, she pulls back her outstretched hand, but Mrs. Ridley has already turned and is marching out of the yard, her back so straight and her neck so stiff there's no doubt about how she feels.

A soft blush is creeping up Jean's neck. Her lips are dry and cracked, and her fingers move across the sheet like little paper butterflies. The dream changes.

She is back in the kitchen with Brian, telling him about her day at work.

"So, that's my day, Brian." But Brian doesn't comment, doesn't repeat what he has said before, doesn't tell her to assert herself and not let people walk all over her. She sits turned away, afraid to see an exasperated look in his face.

"Why don't you talk to me, Brian? We never talk anymore," she whispers, disappointed. Tears trickle down her cheeks. She wipes them with the sleeve of her blouse, and then she turns to look at him.

"No! Brian, please, no…" she moans, and covers her face with her hands.

CHAPTER SIXTEEN

"Rumor is a pipe
Blown by surmises, jealousies, conjectures..."
(Shakespeare, Henry IV)

"*Local man missing, foul play suspected.*"

The Cape Ann Chronicle has somehow—could it possibly be through Mrs. Ridley?—gotten hold of the story. "*A local man has disappeared without a trace. His wife remains in a coma in the hospital after collapsing in the Rockport Library, where she is employed.*"

What follows is standard *Chronicle* fare. Beyond the salacious speculations, obviously put forward by Mrs. Ridley, who is not named in the story, which refers only to an *informed source*, the reporter goes on to suggest that *spousal abuse* might be a possible motive for murder—should a murder have occurred, of course. The implication is obvious: Mrs. Stokes has murdered her abusive husband and stashed his body somewhere. The article goes on to report that Mrs. Stokes is described as "shy and insecure," her husband as "secretive and antisocial," something the reporter theorizes could be a recipe for violence. The article is on the front page and is accompanied by a picture of the missing man. It is the same picture that Annie had seen on the mantel in Jean's kitchen.

"Duncan, look at this!"

Duncan scans the article, and the worried wrinkle between the eyebrows reappears.

"I don't believe it. They've done it again. And the way they couch it, with everything reported as 'alleged,' 'suggested,' or 'possible', there is nothing illegal about any of it. Unethical, to be sure, but nothing they could be sued for or even asked to retract."

"Oh, but it's not just that, Duncan. Look at the picture. I saw that photo on the mantel in Jean's kitchen. How did the paper get hold of it? I locked the door behind me when I left."

"I don't know, Annie. But I don't like this. Not at all. And if you tell the police about that, you'll have to admit to going inside."

"They would just think I had been there to visit before. Or I could say that I saw it when I stuck my head in the door and called for Brian."

"You mean the door that was locked? Anyway, that wouldn't be the whole truth, would it?"

"I'm not on the witness stand."

"Yet."

"I'll tell Judge."

"He'll get mad."

"He'll get over it."

Annie calls Judge, and he gets mad, and she has to hold the phone away from her ear while blue smoke curls out of the receiver.

"But, Judge, I told you I saw that picture when I went through the house. I told you everything I saw."

"You told *me.* But that was before the chief went up there yesterday and found the doors locked, after Mrs. Ridley marched into the RPD to do her civic duty. But Chief Murphy didn't mention any photographs to me. I can't ask him about them, obviously—how would *I* know about them—so there's no way to know whether it was still on the mantel when he went through. I can't imagine how the paper could have gotten the photo any other way than the one you suggest. When I talked to the chief last night, he told me he had not seen any signs of break-in or violence in the house. He confirmed what Mrs. Ridley had reported about empty rooms. At her suggestion, he also checked the basement. Solid cement. Nobody buried down there."

"You could call the paper and ask how they got the photo."

"I could, but I doubt if they'd tell me. I'm sure you noticed that they didn't mention Ridley's name. My guess is that she supplied the photo, but if you saw it and then locked the door when you left, I don't see how she could have acquired it. Or even known it was there, if she'd never been inside."

"Jean would never have asked her in. She's scared to death of Mrs. Ridley. That woman can be very intimidating in order to get what she wants. She makes *me* feel uneasy, and I don't scare as easily as Jean. And Mrs. Ridley couldn't have seen the photo through the window; there's a big cupboard in the way. Oh, she's is evil, I tell you. She probably used witchcraft."

"Now, Annie—"

"I wasn't serious, Judge. By the way, how did the chief get in? I'm sure he didn't break down any doors. Maybe there's a key under the door mat."

"Don't you dare go and check!"

"Then you go."

"I will do no such thing. I might suggest to the chief that he send someone up there to make sure place is secure, and to check for hidden keys. If they find one, I'm sure I'll be able to fish that information out of him."

"You are so clever, Judge. What else did you find out?"

"Not a whole lot, m'dear. I spoke to the physician on duty, Dr. Kim. Simply gave him my name and said that I had just come off the phone with Chief Murphy. That loosened his lips. He told me there has been no upgrading of Jean's condition. Recovery, *if it is to be,* Kim said, could be a lengthy affair, days, weeks, even longer. They can't promise anything. The longer she remains in a coma, the smaller her chance of a satisfactory recovery. He said they would like to perform more tests, but there are some procedures they can't do without locating Mr. Stokes."

"So, nothing new about Brian, then?"

"The chief's put out an APB, of course. But since he now has to consider Stokes a possible victim, instead of a villain, I don't know how aggressively they are pursuing that angle. Now, Annie, dear, let me handle this, would you? Josie is tugging at my sleeve. It appears that breakfast is ready, and then we have to do some shopping. The cupboard is bare, and we are expecting guests tomorrow...or had you forgotten?"

"Not to worry, Judge. Duncan has been going through his list of totally irresistible desserts. I'm sure we won't be disappointed. I just wish I knew what Josie is planning so I could make a salad that would go with it."

"Baaa," Judge says.

• • •

Mrs. Ridley shows up at the library again and doesn't bother to visit Annie's desk this time, but Annie overhears her talking to another patron in the stacks around the corner. Mrs. Ridley has not been afraid to tell people that she was the "informed source" in the *Chronicle*'s article. Suddenly propelled to celebrity status, she now happily expounds on additional theories about where Jean might have hidden her husband's body, the basement theory having been blown.

"There's always Dogtown, of course, especially when you consider that the Stokes' backyard is right in the woods. Or she could have hauled him away in the car—his car is still missing, I understand—and pushed him and the car off a pier, trying to make it look like suicide. There's been a lot of cars going off piers lately, with or without people in them, what with suicides and insurance frauds and all," she points out.

Annie listens and squeezes her eyes shut in disgust. She puts her pen down, closes the book on reference statistics and walks off into Franz's Room. She turns her attention to the Kieran collection, where she reads shelves for a while and restores order among the books. When done, she continues to the mystery section. From there she can see the comings and goings of patrons in the lobby. As usual, a number of Arthur Upfield's books are out on loan. Annie recommends them whenever anyone is looking for a good and different read in mysteries. The remaining volumes of his books are in disorder, flopped this way and that on the shelf, and some lie loosely piled on the little reading table beside the leather wing chair. Annie keeps busy putting the books back in alphabetical order. She is fond of Upfield, whose sleuth Bony, the aborigine Napoleon Bonaparte, is one of her all-time favorites. Annie frequently "takes a trip" to Australia with Bony as her guide. When she finally spies Mrs. Ridley going upstairs—*hopefully to bother Stuart,* she thinks, with an evil smirk—Annie ducks back to the reference desk to finish her paperwork.

When done, she calls Judge to tell him of Mrs. Ridley's further speculations.

"Well, when I talked with the chief just a while ago, Ridley had already gotten to him," Judge reports. "He sounded a little frazzled, frankly. I don't blame him. I think he was trying to decide how much stock to put into her wild ideas. He's sending someone out to check the water at the end of the piers, he said. I'm sure he'll consider a search of the woods at some point, if a more substantial indicator turns up to justify it. Searching all of Dogtown would be costly; he'd need helicopters and extra manpower, and I don't think he feels the time has come yet, but I have a feeling it's in the offing, should Stokes not turn up soon."

CHAPTER SEVENTEEN

"...what manner of speech has escaped the barrier of your teeth?"
(Homer, The Iliad)

Doreen, the hygienist, is tampering with Annie's gums, scraping away at the tartar with gay abandon. Then she taps and picks and pings her teeth, checking every tiny crack and crevice, and jots her findings down on the chart.

"I'll get Doc now, Annie. Just relax."

"Relax? Are you kidding, Doreen? Why don't you people just put me out of my misery? Pull them all out and put in some falsies."

"Come on, Annie, it isn't that bad. Oh, here's Doctor Treadwell now."

"Hello, Annie. How's my favorite librarian?"

"Bet you say that to all of them," Annie says, grumpily.

Treadwell chuckles.

"Let's see, now." The dentist studies her chart and examines every tooth that Doreen has checked off. He does some poking and pricking of his own, digging his tools into every hairline crack.

Annie groans.

"Definite crack in this one. I can see the shadow right through the enamel. Yup, starting to go. No serious decay yet, though. We'll keep a watch on that one."

Doreen nods happily. Every "watched tooth" is a future filling, a source of great contentment for the watchful guard of Annie's pearly-whites.

"Oh, dear." Dr. Treadwell gets to his feet in sheer excitement. "Well, here's a catastrophe waiting to happen. Annie, this one needs immediate care. Half a millimeter of enamel covering a filling that practically takes up the whole tooth, and I can see definite signs of decay in there." Tools and finger come out of her mouth.

"Do we have to do another filling?"

"Afraid not. You're going to need a crown this time."

Annie sighs. This has indeed been a day of sighs. She closes her eyes, and suffers through the rest of his poking and prodding.

"Now, before you go, be sure to make an appointment with Mona. And until I see you, no nuts. Especially almonds." Treadwell knows that almonds are Annie's downfall. They have discussed this issue before, after previous cracked tooth. Doreen takes over, eager to do the final polishing.

"Oh, I almost forgot to tell you, Annie! We got this new machine delivered last week, but we can't open it until the representative is here. I'm just so excited!" Doreen is practically salivating. "I'll be able to get your gums so clean, and then I'll irrigate your deep pockets and kill all the bacteria!" She stops and looks dreamily out the window.

"Whish will lash 'til the nexsh day, when the bactewia gwow back again, wight?" Annie gurgles, the gritty blue tooth polish dribbling out of the corner of her mouth.

"No, no, it takes at least ninety days for the bad bacteria to come back. And since I see you every three months, we can keep them under control." Doreen puts the electric tooth polisher back into Annie's mouth, which silences Annie for the duration of the appointment, when Doreen accompanies her to the front desk.

"Well, Annie, everything go okay?" Mona is well acquainted with Annie's dentist-phobia.

"Sure, Mona. And Doreen's *so* excited about the new equipment you just got in. Says she'll be able to clean and irrigate my deep pockets even better now."

"Are you being sarcastic?" Doreen asks, looking at her suspiciously.

"Oh no, not at all! I love to see people who are enthusiastic about their work!" Annie says. *Only, it's hard to accept someone's enthusiasm about an activity that's going to cause one great pain.* Duncan, for some reason, seems impervious to pain in the dentist's chair. Calm as a cucumber whenever he has to go to the dentist.

While Mona makes Annie's appointment, Annie's eyes travel to the file rack behind the secretary, row upon row of manila folders with colorful tabs. Annie suddenly has a brainstorm. *A dentist.* Maybe a dentist in Louisville would know the Stokes family and be able to give her the name of any relatives who might still be living there? She will look into it.

"Your appointment is the same time, next week."

With some free time left on her hands, Annie decides to take a walk in Dogtown. Just a nature walk, to recover from the ordeal in the dentist's chair. She intends to put Jean's situation and Brian's disappearance out of her mind completely. On an impulse, she calls Sally.

"Great! I love our Dogtown rambles! Want to pick me up or shall I come get you?"

"Oh...well, I know how you love my car, Sal...so, come and get me, then." Annie's old Chevy is doing fine, for an old crate, but Sally has a long list of complaints about it: the passenger seat can't be adjusted, the engine whines and sputters, the muffler makes an ominous sound, the window won't roll down...Annie smiles. Anyway, Sally's SUV will take them further into the woods.

CHAPTER EIGHTEEN

"We shall not cease from exploration
And the end of all our exploring
Will be to arrive where we started
And know the place for the first time."
(T. S. Eliot, The Four Quartets)

Dogtown, at about 3600 acres, covers a large area of the island, *with plenty of room to hide a body,* Annie can't stop herself from thinking. There are several swamps, a large moor, and a couple of water reservoirs that keep the islanders with fresh water; numerous quarries, and a multitude of streams. The old Commons Road winds its way leisurely across the landscape, avoiding the more difficult terrain. Trails and footpaths crisscross the place, some listed on the local maps, others not.

They drive in as far as they can along one of the old fire trails. When the terrain gets too rough even for Sally's big SUV, they park between the trees on the side of the road. Sally locks the car with her little remote. Annie rolls her eyes.

"Boy, you sure love your hi-tech gadgets, don't you?"

Sally smiles. Annie always tries to make fun of the practical conveniences that most people have gotten used to.

"You should have been a pioneer, or one of those survivalists. Do you ever yearn to go west, young lady? You'd fit right in with the other cowboys."

"Pfft. You're all becoming dependent on those things, you know? Can you even remember my phone number?"

"I don't need to. You're on my call menu. Number 2, actually, Matt's Number 1, of course."

"Okay, say you lost your phone or the battery died. So did your car. You're on the turnpike, calling from one of those quickie food stops that look so alike all over the country that you could be anywhere and still find your way to the bathroom. You're standing at a pay-phone, trying to reach me. What's my number?"

"Eh, 546...something, something."

"Hah. See?"

"Well, you've got a cell phone yourself."

"Yes, but I won't program it. My memory is in my brain, not in my gadget."

It's Sally's turn to roll her eyes.

"For a technophobe, I'm surprised you use a computer."

"Oh, that's totally different. I love my computer, except when it balks at me or moves things around without asking my permission. No, I'm just talking about all those small, useless things that people become dependent on. Then, and always when you need them the most, they don't work because the power went or the battery died or something. People come to me at the reference desk all the time with their problems. *'Oh, Miss Quitnot, what do I do? I accidentally erased my memory and lost all my phone numbers,'* or sometimes it's appointments, important notes, or photos. But I do feel more empathy for them than for the Blackberry thumb people or all those MBAs who drive BMWs and keep their money in IRAs and can't go anywhere without their IPods or I Pads or whatever the current fad gadget is, which they can manipulate in their sleep, I'm sure—"

"Okay, peace already. Are we going to get lost today?" Sally asks hopefully. She's in the mood for adventure, secure in the knowledge that Annie will find the way back. Eventually. Even without a GPS gadget.

Annie has gotten lost many times in Dogtown. She still enjoys leaving the trail, but getting lost is actually becoming a challenge, as she knows the place too well. Her parents used to take her blueberrying on the moor and cranberrying out in Briar Swamp, the biggest of the swamps. In those days, she had never been allowed to go out in the swamp alone. Parts of it are wet and boggy. Once out in the middle, surrounded by tall grass and shrubby hummocks, one can only see a few yards in any direction. But her parents had encouraged her to find her way around on the trails. "If you don't stray too far from the Commons Road, you won't lose your way. Worst case, you'll end up in Gloucester," her father used to tell her. "If you do get lost, just pick a direction and stick to it. After a couple of hours, you should be out of the woods." True, but only after trekking through myriads of swamps and prickerbushes and across brooks and around quarries and other water holes.

Before her parents bought the Hannah Jumper house in downtown Rockport, and while they still lived in Pigeon Cove, Annie had considered Dogtown her backyard. It had only taken her a few minutes to reach one of the paths that led into the woods. They had moved when the magnificent new Denghausen Library opened, and the Story branch library in the Cove closed, along with the old Carnegie Library downtown. Many people still miss the branch library, and if it weren't for Maureen, the outreach librarian, many of the elderly in Pigeon Cove wouldn't have steady access to fresh reading material. All they have to do is call Maureen, and she'll bring them whatever their hearts desire, in whatever shape or form they need: large print, audio book, tape, or standard book format. Maureen is older than most of the people she serves and will be hard to replace when she retires.

"Boy, will you look at that!" Annie points ahead.

…, many people will only walk in Dogtown with a companion or one of the organized walking groups, but Annie stubbornly refuses to give up the privilege of walking alone in the wilds.

They have to bend down a little to get through an evergreen bower of shiny-leaved mountain laurel, prolific here at the southern end of the swamp. When in bloom, they drop their flowers into the inky black pools at the edge, pools with islands of green moss that Annie calls "Emerald Isles." In early summer, the little star-shaped laurel flowers float around in the pools among reflections of the clouds, mirroring the cosmos. But now it's fall, and only dried brown seed-clusters adorn the evergreens today. As they close in on the swamp, they run into a mess of hobblebush, whose long, spindly branches reach for the ground and root themselves, setting a trap for the innocent passerby.

"Watch out, Sal," Annie says and points down at the roots.

They step around the trap. Tall and slender witch hazel, whose curious yellow flowers are just now sprouting from the branches, stand in a row next to the old, mossy stone dam that keeps the tannin-rich swamp water from flowing into the island's water shed.

"Scarlet tupelo." Annie points.

A few hundred yards into the woods the trail has been blocked. This has happened repeatedly over the past few years, especially in this same place, and Annie angrily starts to remove the offensive obstruction. Rubble, metal bars, and chains, carefully camouflaged with dead tree branches and thorny vines, have been dragged to the spot and heaped across the path. Annie tosses them aside with a lot of clanging noise. Sally stays out of the way, safely hidden behind a tree, in case whoever did this shows up carrying a shotgun. But Annie doesn't care if anyone hears her. Bring him on! Development is eating into Dogtown, one narrow swath at a time, and people who move into the outlying areas of the woodlands don't want anyone "infringing on their privacy." But these are public paths, right-of-ways since time immemorial, and Annie defends them, jaws clenched. The vicious, thorny cat-briar, "the plant from hell," as some insist, has scratched her hands and arms bloody, which only serves to make her more irate. At least she has found no dead body hidden among the rubble.

Energized by anger, she continues along the trail. Sally follows close behind, casting anxious glances around her, but they are alone in the woods. On the other side of the obstruc-

Gunilla Caulfield

edge of the quarry, someone has left a bundle. Annie points it out to Sally. Taking the narrow path along the edge of the quarry, they pick their way down.

"That's Bella's bag, Sally. Recognize the smell?"

The black nylon bag sits on top of one of the big flat ledges used by sun worshippers in the summer. This corner of the quarry used to be a favorite place for skinny dippers years ago, but it is too frequently patrolled these days. They look around. It's a little cold for people like Bella to be living in the woods, so what would she be doing here? Her nightly ablutions?

"Well, we'd better leave it in case she comes back for it."

They find Bella's bowler a few hundred yards away, and Annie picks it up, but puts it down again.

"She might leave her bag for a while, but she'd never part with that hat," Annie says, looking around. Where could she be? It's getting dark. Annie has a bad feeling.

"Come on, Sally."

Without another word they start running back down toward Sally's car.

"But I forgot about the mint jelly," she says, dismayed.

"Not to worry! It just so happens that a little bird told me, and I made a salad to go with the lamb." Annie uncovers her great salad platter, generously afflicted with sprigs of mint. There are olives, too, of course, the little Nicoise kind, along with grape tomatoes, baby gherkins and thinly sliced toasted almonds. *Oh, will they crack my tooth and send me back to the dentist?* Annie thinks.

"Little bird, was it? Not this great owl of mine, then?" Josie says, giving Judge a suspicious look. Judge tries to look owlish, opening his eyes wide.

"Hoot, hoot" he says.

After the dinner plates have been cleared off the table, Josie pours the coffee and Duncan uncovers his "fabulous" dessert. They all look at it in astonishment. There is a slight silence, until Judge clears his throat.

"What happened to it?" he asks.

"What *is* it?" Josie tries a different tack.

"Prune soufflé." Duncan sounds defensive.

"I thought a soufflé was supposed to be puffy," Annie says, looking a little concerned.

"Yes, and that people were supposed be sitting around waiting for it to be baked and rushed to the table before it deflated," Josie adds.

"Looks like this one got deflated," Judge decides.

Duncan laughs derisively.

"O ye of little faith," he says.

The prunes are soft and juicy, like restored plums, and the soufflé itself is more like a chewy meringue than the standard, airy creation.

"So, is this a British thing, then?" Judge asks.

"Not at all. Dad had a Swedish housekeeper, and she used to make this for us every Sunday. One of Dad's favorites, it was." Anytime Duncan talks or thinks about England, he begins to sound like a Brit. When his American mother died in a car accident in Iowa, Duncan had gone to live with the father he had never met, a professor at Oxford. Duncan had finished his schooling in London and taught there himself for a while, before switching to a library career and returning to the States.

"Well," Judge admits, "I regret my lack of faith. How much groveling would it take to have a chance at seconds?"

Duncan, with a great display of condescension, dishes out seconds for everyone. And after they are through with dessert and have drunk the last of the coffee, there is nothing for it but to tackle the elephant in the room. Just then the phone rings.

"The police have confirmed that there's a car in the quarry, apparently containing a body. They'll pull it out as soon as they can get the equipment up there in the morning. They didn't find Bella, though." Judge sits down and takes a large swig of coffee.

Annie covers her eyes with her hands. *Please, make it not be Brian. And Bella, what could have happened to her?*

"Chief's been up to the Stokes' house again. Had a forensic crew go through it. Yellow-taped the property. Barred the garage doors, which was how the chief and Hale got in. Took possession of the spare key, which was left under a rock by the back entrance. So now we know how the photo found its way to the paper, don't we? Pending forensic results and getting the car out of the quarry, there's nothing more to be done right now. Jean's still under guard. The search for Brian is on hold until the car is retrieved and the body positively identified. However, the chief seemed to feel that they've found their man. Their victim, I mean. He didn't say so, but I think he is confident that they have their murderer, too."

"Even if the body in the quarry *is* Brian's, that doesn't mean that Jean did it," Annie says. "Who knows what dangerous government business Brian might be involved in? All this secrecy. What if he's in a department that deals with crime or narcotics or even terrorism? That could also explain why he never wanted to be seen. And if that's the case, he could have been killed by a hit man."

Eyes roll discreetly, and Judge clears his throat.

"Well, well. We must certainly keep an open mind."

"What about Bella? Did they just stop looking for her?" Annie asks.

"The chief says there isn't necessarily any connection…"

"Unless she was a witness," Duncan says. Annie looks at him gratefully. At least someone else cares.

"But maybe she just went there for a swim?" Judge shrugs his shoulders.

"There's ice at the edges of the quarries!" Annie objects. "Besides, I didn't see her today. She's in the library every day this time of year. We're one of her usual stops to get out of the cold. So, she's disappeared at the very least."

"Have you heard anything more from the hospital about Jean?" Duncan says, trying to avoid further fruitless speculation.

Judge shakes his head. "Her condition remains unchanged, according to Dr. Kim. That is not an encouraging sign. Dr. Kim feels she should have come around by now, since they have found no convincing physical reason for her remaining in a coma. But the human brain is still an enigma in many ways, he pointed out. There is so much we still don't know, so much we are unable to predict."

Annie has been quiet for a while. Something in the back of her mind is nagging her, and suddenly she knows what it is. *Of course. It's so obvious.*

"Oh, but now I remember! Bella was in the library the day *after* Jean collapsed and was taken to the hospital," she says, "so if Bella disappeared because she was scared after being a witness to the killing and the car being dumped into the quarry, Jean would have had to rise out of her coma to commit it. *But,* could it mean that Bella *did* witness it, *when Jean was already in the hospital?* If the killing of whoever's in the car took place *after* Jean went into the hospital, it would obviously have to mean that Bella witnessed *someone other than Jean* commit the crime. You know, some hit man, like I said before..."

"Except now this purported witness can't help us, since she's disappeared. I don't think we're getting anywhere with this, my dear. Let's wait until they pull the car out. Anyway, the chief said they'd continue the search for Bella in the morning," Judge says, rising to put an end to the discussion. "I suggest we move into the living room."

A small snifter of cognac wouldn't hurt. Maybe they can end the evening on a different note.

CHAPTER TWENTY

"Right as an aspen leef she gan to quake."
(Chaucer, Troilus and Criseyde)

The sun hits the yellow roses on Jean's bedside table, spreading a sweet scent in the hospital room and prompting another dream.

"Jeanie-girl, what's the matter? You crying and Mama slamming doors and storming out of the house. What's upset you?"

"Oh, Papa." She is sobbing too hard to continue, and Papa puts his big strong arms around her just like he'd done when she was a little girl.

"Come now, tell me about it."

"Mama says I mustn't ever see Brian again. She says we're first cousins, and it's wrong. But, Papa, I love him..." A fresh set of sobs set in.

Papa leads her to the sofa, and they sit down. When she is calmer, he gives her a searching look and takes her hands. She has taken the ring off; it lies hidden in one of her bureau drawers, wrapped in a sock.

"Jeanie, you're a big girl now...no, a woman. Eighteen, which is how old your mama was when I married her. You are old enough to know the truth. Come with me." He leads her over to the big gilt mirror that hangs on the living room wall. The immaculately polished surface reflects a roomful of plush furniture. There is a walnut coffee table, books and newspapers scattered around a heavy bronze vase filled with yellow roses from Papa's rose garden, and a great fieldstone fireplace with all the family photographs on the mantel. In the mirror image she can also see the picture window full of Mama's flowering plants,

and the great tulip trees that line the street outside. They look into the mirror together, she and Papa, he with his arm around her shoulders.

"What do you see, Jean?"

"You and me, Papa. Oh, I look awful, all red in the face."

"You look as beautiful as always. Look at those big, violet eyes. Now, look at mine. What color are they?"

"They are brown, Papa."

"And Mama's?"

"She has brown eyes, too."

"Did you ever wonder why yours aren't brown?"

"I never thought about it, Papa."

"Well, Jean, let's go sit down, and I'll tell you why."

And now Papa tells her the last thing in the world that she would ever want to hear: that he is not really her father. Her mama had been pregnant when they married, but not by him. A stranger from out of town had come in like a whirlwind and turned Mama's head, and then taken off, never to be heard from again. And Papa had rescued Mama by marrying her and, although there had been a small scandal when it was found out that she had been a pregnant bride, it was nothing compared to what it would have been had the truth come out.

"I loved your mother, you see. The rest didn't matter to me. And I love you. Since the day you were born, you have been my daughter, and I thank the man with the violet eyes for giving you to me."

She starts sobbing again and clings to him, hugging him desperately.

"Oh, Papa."

"There, now, girl. Stop your bawling. Everything is the same as it ever was. Mama and I both love you."

They remain quiet for a while, sitting in the soft green sofa, holding hands.

"But, Papa, if Brian isn't really my first cousin, why can't I see him?"

"Now you listen to me, my girl. Your mama never wanted it to be known that you are not mine. The scandal would have killed her. It still would. That's why."

"But I love him. I will never want anyone else."

"If that's so, Jeanie, you surely have to follow your heart. You may tell Brian what I've told you, but he mustn't let on to anyone else in the family, because it would cause your mama a world of grief. She'd never get over it. One day, if things go the way you want, you two will just have to disappear from here and go and live somewhere else. It will be the only way. I will miss you when that day comes, but I will always love you, no matter where you are."

Jean moans as though she is in pain, but there is no one in the room to hear her. Her arms twitch, and the blanket shifts and slides off her chest. The thin hands flutter momentarily and settle again. Tears squeeze out under trembling eyelids. A while later, when Grace stops in, Jean lies as immobile as before. Grace pulls up the blanket to cover the patient before taking her pulse, which is slow and steady. Grace sees the bouquet of yellow roses from the library staff on the bedside table and rolls the table away from the bed a little, so the sweet fragrance won't disturb the patient. She sits by Jean's bedside for a few moments, holding her hand.

"Wake up, Jean. Come back to us," she whispers.

Instead, the patient seems to be slipping away from them. Her face looks peaceful, but so far away.

CHAPTER TWENTY-ONE

"Once more the engine of her thoughts began"
(Shakespeare, Venus and Adonis)

Duncan has gone for the Sunday paper. Annie sits down and decides to try a phone number from her list. Louisville looks like a small town, not far from Knoxville. Maybe the dentist has an office right in his home.

"Dr. Bromfield? This is Miss Quitnot. I wonder if you can help me. I'm looking for a man named Brian Stokes, and I was wondering if he is or ever was a patient of yours?"

"Well...Miss Quitnot, is it? What's this for? I don't usually give out information about my patients over the phone."

Dr. Bromfield must have been born and educated somewhere else; he doesn't sound much like a southerner. A slight twang, at the most.

"Oh, I understand. It's an emergency, though. You see, his wife is in the hospital, and we haven't been able to reach him. Her condition is quite serious. Is there any way you could help us?"

"Oh, dear. Well, let me have a look. The name is familiar. I've had several patients named Stokes over the years."

It takes some time, but he gets back on the line and says, "Yes, I did have a patient by the name of Brian Stokes, but that was over twenty years ago. There's a note here that says he went into the service at that time. He never sent for his records or X-rays. I suppose when they enter the service they have a whole new set made. I have no current address for him."

"You've been very kind, Dr. Bromfield. I appreciate your help." Annie is ready to hang up, when she hears Dr. Bromfield clear his throat and start to speak again, a little hesitantly.

"I recall that Brian Stokes had a brother named Mitchell, who also was a patient of mine. I believe he still lives in town, but I haven't seen him for some years. And if I remember correctly, there was a sister, too, Maisie, who retired to Florida some years back. She was the oldest of the Stokes children. Married a fellow named Goodwin, I believe. She was never a patient of mine. She and her parents went to old Doc Hartman, who passed a good many years back. I don't know if that would be of any help to you. I hope you may find Mr. Stokes and all will turn out well."

Annie does a quick double-check to make sure she has all the information.

"Thank you so much, Dr. Bromfield."

So, another connection to Mitchell Stokes. That seems to seal that, all the pieces fit...Annie shakes her head in frustration. She hears the door open, and Duncan walks in, tossing the paper on the table.

"Ready for a cup of coffee?"

CHAPTER TWENTY-TWO

"Atoms or systems into ruin hurl'd
And now a bubble burst, and now a world."
(Alexander Pope, An Essay on Man)

Jean is deep in her dream world.

Papa is leading the way. She can see the river through the grove of trees. It's high summer and still hot, even though it's late in the day. They have just finished dinner and are out on one of their evening walks while Mama takes her usual after dinner nap. They are walking in a hayfield, on a narrow, grassy path that winds down toward the riverbank. The dry, knee-high grass makes a swishing sound as they walk. Cattails and reeds grow in the ditch that runs alongside the path, and a frog croaks and hops into the water when they approach. After a while they reach the edge of the trees and walk into the cool shade. Papa slows down to wait for her. She struggles to get her nerve up.

"Papa? I've got something to tell you."

"Yes, my girl, what is it?"

"I'm leaving home." Her throat closes up. She can't bear to continue.

Papa has slowed down, and half turns around to face her. "Oh, Jeanie-girl, I'm so happy for you..."

*His silhouette is outlined by the river, the beautiful green stretch of the Tennessee River that flows by in the background. She can hear the rushing and clucking of water over rocks from the shallows around the bend. She can't see Papa's face, even though he is turned toward her now. The light is coming up from the river, through the trees, and all she sees is the shape of him, tall and broad-shouldered...*and then *he seems to recede, to disappear backwards, and she realizes that he is toppling, falling over like a great oak felled in a storm.*

"Papa," she cries. She reaches him in a few steps, but he is down on the ground now, on his back, arms flung wide. His eyes are wide open, and they stare at her.

"Papa, are you all right?" she cries, but she knows he is not.

He moans, and his lips move, but she can't hear what he is trying to say. She puts her arms across him and holds him tight. She feels him take a trembling breath, and then he goes slack and lies still.

"Oh, Papa, don't die!" she cries. She howls, she hugs him desperately, and then she leaves him and runs back across the fields, toward the house.

"I killed him; I killed him," Jean whispers.

Grace takes a step closer, leans over her patient, and puts her ear over her mouth, but Mrs. Stokes has nothing more to say. Shocked, the nurse calls Dr. Kim to come and check on Mrs. Stokes. He walks in hurriedly, looking first at the patient, who lies as immobile as ever, then at Grace.

"What? I thought maybe she was awake."

"No, Doctor Kim, but her pulse was racing, and her heart was beating so fast, I thought maybe something was going on. Her arms were moving, sort of shaking back and forth. I was afraid she was starting to have convulsions."

"Let me have a look. Did you touch her?"

"I…I just took her hand for a moment…" Grace sounds anxious.

"Fine, fine."

When he has finished checking the patient, he walks over to the window and looks out. It's not a pleasant view, only a blank wall straight ahead and a narrow alley for delivery vans below, lit with strong flood lights in the dark.

"She doesn't *want* to wake up," he mumbles, talking to himself.

Grace looks at him, amazed.

"I know." She hesitates, then she blurts it out quickly, before she has time to change her mind, "Dr. Kim, she whispered something. I'm not sure I heard it right, but I think she said '*I killed him*'...I may be wrong, though."

Dr. Kim eyes the nurse for a moment. "Why didn't you tell me this right away?"

"What if I made a mistake? I did hear her whisper something, but it was only a whisper, and I couldn't swear to what she said."

"I should call the police. I think I'll call Judge Bradley first. How late are you working tonight, Grace?"

"Until 11."

"Fine. Don't leave the hospital without seeing me first."

"No, Dr. Kim. I hope I was wrong. I wish I hadn't heard her..."

"Grace, you did the right thing. Now, let's leave the rest to Judge Bradley, he'll know what to do."

CHAPTER TWENTY-THREE

"Blind and naked ignorance
Delivers brawling judgments, unashamed,
On all things all day long."
(Tennyson, "Merlin and Vivien")

Judge had been right, as usual. The town is abuzz with the goings-on at Steel Derrick Quarry, or just plain *Steel,* as it's known by the locals, and Mrs. Ridley is gloating beyond all measure.

"Of course you all know I told the chief right from the start that she had probably driven Stokes over a cliff. He deserved it, I'm sure. She always seemed so nervous and skittish; you all must have noticed that. I'm sure he intimidated her. Don't know for sure whether it was physical abuse, but everyone knows that mental abuse can do just as much harm. But I guess she got him back in the end."

Mrs. Ridley is holding court on the library steps, waiting for the doors to open. It's Sunday, but the Rockport Library has a long history of being the only library in the consortium to keep open on Sundays. Annie is able to hear Ridley's grating voice through the windows.

Oh, why did I ever call Judge? she thinks.

• • •

By the time the equipment is in place, a few gawkers have gathered at Steel. Since there is no legal way to drive to this spot, everyone who arrives has had a long trek through the woods in dismal weather. The islanders have risen to a drizzly, cold, and windy November morning. Well, it's not hard to understand why people might prefer staying in their cozy cottages with the scanner on. Annie is standing alone under a tree, keeping a respectful distance. She is not looking forward to what is to come, but she considers it her moral obligation to be present, lending support to a colleague who can't be there herself. She would also like her presence to be read as a sign that she does not believe Jean capable of the sort of crime that Mrs. Ridley has suggested. A number of people in town have jumped on the Ridley bandwagon, and they are undoubtedly sitting by their scanners, sipping coffee, and waiting eagerly for confirmation.

A large area up on the high ledge, where the crane is located, has been taped off, and anyone who tries to approach the cordon is swiftly waved away. Judge has managed to get inside and is chatting casually with Chief Murphy. Mrs. Ridley arrives and tries to also get inside the taped off area, but she gets abruptly shooed away by Officer Elwell. She stays nearby, inching closer when she thinks no one is watching, and Elwell finally walks up to her, fists on hips, chin out.

"Stay away or you'll be sitting in the cruiser, ma'am. This is police business."

A diver has been sent down to take some pictures. The chief wants to make sure that evidence doesn't get lost in the hoisting process. Finally, the diver surfaces and waves that he is done. He swims briskly over toward the flat rock area, where a few onlookers have gathered, mostly women.

The crane rumbles to life, and two other divers swim down to attach the cables and harness to the vehicle. Once the divers are safely out of the way, the hoisting begins. The crane rocks and shudders as the vehicle jangles loose from the ledge, far down under the water's surface. A woman screams when the full weight of the salvage is on the cables and it looks like the crane is about to topple. It has been properly counterweighted, however, and slowly brings up its load. As the vehicle breaks the surface, the onlookers get a glimpse of a shoulder and the back of a neck. A pale ear presses against the driver's side window. The cabin is full of water, like an oversized aquarium, with the body floating around inside. When an arm lifts and seems to wave to them, the same woman who screamed before screams again, and covers her face. The woman is too far away for Annie to recognize her, especially since she is wearing a hooded parka and a muffler tucked up over her mouth. The crane whines and grinds, straining under its load. The body flops out of sight as the crane lifts the vehicle free and water gushes out through the undercarriage.

Once the car has been placed on the ledge, at a safe distance from the cliff's edge, the harness and cables are removed and the driver's side door opened. The remaining water pours out. A man with a camera tries to clamber up along the rocks to the ledge to get a better view, but he's quickly waved back down. Within minutes the body bag is loaded and whisked away, and the gawkers disperse, some of them a little disappointed, perhaps, at not being able to get a good, if gruesome, look at the victim. As they disappear down the path, the forensic team is left to do its preliminary work undisturbed. Later, the vehicle, a black Jeep Cherokee, will be lifted onto a flatbed and taken away for further examination.

Annie, walking around the taped-off area in order to reach the path, notices that the Jeep's license plates had been removed, maybe to suggest that the vehicle was stolen, in case it should ever be found and brought up. Of course, if it had government plates it would have been too easy to trace, unlike a lot of stolen cars that have been outfitted with fake plates. The fact that the vehicle got caught on the ledge must have been unexpected. She wonders if whoever pushed the car had stayed around long enough to walk up to the edge for a look. There are several stickers in the windows, but nothing that she is able to recognize at the distance. Most of the time people plaster bragging stickers all over their vehicles, or just parking stickers from wherever they live or work. Some Rockporters show off their frugality by not removing the previous year's parking sticker, just plastering the new one on beside it, as if to indicate, "*yes folks, this is how old my car is.*" Annie's old Chevy has a veritable necklace of stickers around the rear window. In her case, it's to show people how much she loves that old crate. It's a *historical artifact,* she claims, and when it croaks, maybe she'll donate it to a museum. Today she has come up here on foot. When she notices Judge walking toward his car, she hurries to get to him before he drives away.

"Wait, Judge!"

She gets in, and Judge takes off, driving too fast on the uneven, rocky trail. They bounce violently up and down while Annie tries in vain to fasten her seat belt.

"Wow, Judge, easy! I know teenagers who drive slower than this," she complains.

"What's the matter? Queasy stomach?" Judge asks.

Annie has to admit to an uneasy feeling, but it is more likely a result of the scene they have just left. Judge himself had been standing right there when the body was hauled out, but no doubt he has seen worse. Annie had been grateful to be at a distance. She finally manages to engage the belt buckle.

"Did you recognize him?" she asks.

"No, I'm afraid not. Face was very swollen, all mangled. Unrecognizable, I would say. He wasn't strapped in. Could have happened when the truck hit the water, I guess. Maybe he fell against the steering wheel; the windshield wasn't broken.

We'll find out. If he drowned, that's probably how it happened. If not, well, then he was dead before he went over the edge, and who knows what might have caused the injuries. Anyway, I only know what he looked like from that photo in the paper. The Ridley woman was leaning across the tape, pointing at him and shouting, 'that's him, that's him,' but I'll wait for a positive ID. That's the only thing we can do at the moment," he says, sounding somewhat discouraged.

They have gotten down to Granite Street, and Annie decides she needs a little time before going to the library.

"Judge, why don't you let me off here. I could use some fresh air and a little time to think."

Annie gets out and walks along Granite Street, crossing Keystone Bridge before turning left onto Beach Street, the shortest route to the library. There she sees Esa, who is also on the way to work, and joins him. They speedwalk past Back Beach, which lies open to the sea. It's getting colder, almost feels cold enough to snow, and stiff, horizontal wind gusts aim stinging sleet at their eyes. She is sorry now to have left the warmth of Judge's car.

"Wow, it's cold," Esa says, covering his face with a woolly mitten.

Annie thinks of Bella, without her hat and whatever extra clothes she keeps in that bag of hers.

"Esa, do you know where Bella is staying?" she asks.

Esa looks around as if to be certain nobody is listening.

"Miss Annie, you can't tell nobody, but she said she found a way to get into the old Tool Company. There's even a place in there where she lights a fire. She says it's safe 'cause that's where they had fires when they worked in the forge. She's even brought blankets there to sleep on, she says." Esa puts the mitten back in front of his face to protect himself from the biting wind.

"Esa, I just remember there's something I have to do. Let's hurry up, so we don't catch cold!" Annie says, and Esa nods as they trot up Beach Knoll, he first and Annie right behind. He pulls his hood tightly around his head for the next open stretch along Front Beach. The tide is on the way in. At low tide, the sandy stretch of Front Beach is walkable all the way over to Lumber Wharf, but now the waves are rolling in, smashing up against the stone wall.

When they get to the library, a knot of people has collected on the portico, waiting for the library to open. Mrs. Ridley is among them, holding court again, claiming to be the one to have identified the victim.

"It was Stokes, I just know it. His face was all bashed in, but I had a good view from the side. That wavy dark hair, and the jaw and ear, well, that was all I needed. It was him all right, and I told the chief so. She did him in, that Mrs. Stokes, just like I said. And did you see today's paper? The police are looking for a possible witness..."

"Let's go in the back way," Annie whispers, and Esa nods.

After heating a mugful of coffee, black as tar and about as tasty, Annie heads for her desk and tries to find relief in paperwork. There's enough of that, to be sure. She bulldozes through most of it before lunch, trying not to pay attention to a gaggle of patrons who hang around listening to the morning's gossip, which includes a breathless eye witness account by someone who had been up at Steel. Putting the remaining paperwork aside until later, Annie continues working on a list of recently published reference books to request at the next staff meeting. She starts by going through the latest *New York Review of Books*, looking for anything that she might have missed.

As soon as the noon signal blares from the fire station, she jogs home to take Gussie out for a walk on Front Beach. Gussie gets carried most of the way, being elderly and a little fragile.

They make their way down through the alley next to Toad Hall Bookstore.

A flock of seagulls come in for a landing and settle in a tight little group up on the sandy lee end of the beach. Annie puts Gussie down, and he works diligently at herding seagulls for a while. They only laugh at him, "*hwaa-hwaa-hwaa,*" while trotting back and forth, heads up, beaks wide open, taunting him. Finally Gussie flops down on the wet sand, exhausted and panting, and Annie brings him home. She rubs him dry with a towel, and he proudly hops into his basket. Even at two inches off the floor, it's a brave hop for an elderly dachshund. As Annie is walking out the door, Sally calls and asks them over for dinner.

"Lobstah," she says. She knows that's all she needs to say, and Annie is only too happy to accept. She'd take any distraction offered, but what can beat lobsters?

"What can we bring?"

"A bottle of wine?"

"Sure thing. We'll be there."

Annie checks what she jokingly refers to as "Hannah's likker locker." A bottle of red wine, but that won't go with the lobster. A Pinot Grigio would have been nice, but no such luck. There's a cheap bottle of Zinfandel, which Annie used to keep on hand for girls' night, mostly a thing of the past now. Oh, well, it will have to do. Doubtless the men will sniff scornfully at the sight, but they'll drink it. She puts it in the refrigerator to cool. Now she has to run to get back to the library on time.

Snow has been forecast. The islanders had launched a full-scale attack on the supermarkets at the crack of dawn. They had loaded their carts with enough bread to last through Christmas, raided the canned goods shelves, and bought up every sterno, flashlight and battery in sight. Now they have come to the library to stock up on reading materials, high on the list of life's necessities in Rockport. Winter can be of long duration, and the islanders often get cut off from the mainland after severe storms.

Anyone on Cape Ann who lived through the '78 storm remembers the weeks that followed: no power, stores closed, streets caved in. The National Guard prowled the exits for anyone who thought they could make it off the island to some mainland shopping center. A wave washed a large colonial home into Old Harbor, to float until it disintegrated there among refrigerators and cars, one of them a Thunderbird. A small cottage on Beach Street was deposited in the middle of the street. What most people didn't know was that the cottage had first been taken by a wave and brought out into the middle of Sandy Bay before being brought back by another wave and lifted back up onto the street. Cars were buried under the snow all along Route 128. Families were kept apart. Close friendships were made when people opened their homes to those who didn't have a fireplace or a woodstove. No doubt some friendships were also tested, as too much closeness can expose sides of people you never expect to see. Pets were lost, some found frozen to death when the snow melted, some taken in by strangers and returned after the storm. The week after the storm, one man went to shovel out his car in the yard. When he got the rear window cleared, he found himself face to face with his own irate cat, which was trying to claw his way through the window, hissing and scratching. The creature was a pitiful sight, skinny, fur standing on end, and when the man let him out of the car, the cat took off like a bullet. Fortunately, the snow was deep, and the cat was so weak he didn't even make it to the gate before the man caught him. No doubt a tender scene was played out inside the house, the man offering his poor cat some scraps of food and water and a rubdown. Doubtless also, the man had a second shock waiting for him the next time he got back into his car.

CHAPTER TWENTY-FOUR

"If you can't give me your word of honor,
will you give me your promise?"
(Samuel Goldwyn quote, from Alva Johnston, The Great Goldwyn)

By the time Annie reaches the parking lot, the drizzle has turned to sleet. Inside, Penny and Marie are busy at the circulation desk. Penny looks flustered, as Marie has her own line of patrons to contend with.

Annie, already late, shakes the wet snow off her coat and drapes it over a radiator before hurrying toward her desk. Duncan is waiting for her there, pacing back and forth in the reference area. As he walks past the corner of her desk, Annie sees him eyeing it with a look of mild astonishment. She has to admit that it looks even messier than usual. He bends over to read the small quote she recently taped to a corner of her desktop:

"If a cluttered desk is a sign of a cluttered mind,
Of what, then, is an empty desk?" Albert Einstein.

A self-serving excuse, maybe, but Annie works best surrounded by a little omnium gatherum. When Duncan hears her footsteps he turns around. He is not smiling, and her heart sinks.

"What? Jean?"

"No. We can't talk here. Come on up to my office."

Annie asks Marie to buzz her if anyone comes in with a reference question, before following Duncan up the stairs. On the second landing, she walks by the windows of the technical services office, where Clare sits hunched over her keyboard cataloging a stack of new fiction.

Annie misses her old, easy friendship with Clare. The two of them had grown up together and been close until Carlo's death. After Carlo, so much in Annie's life had changed and fallen by the wayside—the friendship with Clare being one of them—and things had never been the same again. Of all her colleagues in the library, only Clare and Stuart had let her down, actually believing that she had murdered Carlo. How could *Clare* have believed Annie guilty of murder? That was still hard to swallow. Not too long ago, Annie would have asked Clare, as her oldest friend, to be her maid of honor, but instead she had asked Sally, who would never be sneaky or stab a friend in the back.

Clare looks up as Annie walks by. Annie smiles and waves. Clare sticks her head out the door.

"Hey, Annie, feel like going over to the coffee shop when you have a break?"

"Sounds great," Annie says, turning away, eager to get to Duncan's office.

"Perfect. Just have to finish logging in some recent acquisitions. Look at this stack of Large Prints. I know they won't fit on the shelves. We're going to have to do some serious weeding..."

"Wow. Here we are, in our new, beautiful, huge library, and we already have to weed in order to fit more books in. Well, got to run, Clare. The boss wants to see me... See you in half an hour." She hurries off before Clare can think of anything else to say to keep her there.

Duncan's door is open, as always. His desk is neater than Annie's, but not by much, she notes with satisfaction. She flops down in the chair across from him.

"Had a call from Judge." Duncan starts right in. "They haven't identified the body yet. Chief's still convinced that it's Brian, but it may take some time to determine beyond doubt, and we have to wait for results. The man didn't drown, though. He was dead before the car went into the quarry, that much has been established. So it wasn't suicide, anyway. Judge went with the chief and had a look at the body in the morgue. The face was bashed in pretty badly. Would have taken some strength, or else he was caught by surprise, maybe in bed, Judge figured. They found wood splinters in the wound. Didn't find anything in the car or up around the quarry that might have been used as a tool. A tree branch or a piece of firewood, maybe. Not the usual baseball bat, which probably wouldn't splinter."

"Did Judge have any news about Jean?"

"No. You know, Annie, I get the feeling that Judge may be holding back on something there. He hems and haws a lot. Seems to be more worried about Jean than before. I don't know whether it's her medical condition or the possibility that she's guilty that's worrying him. Anyway, he sent Josie over to the hospital. Judge called ahead to say she was coming; apparently, they were going to let her in to see the patient, with the guard present, of course. You could give her a call. She may be back home by now. Maybe she has some information." Annie nods and dials Judge's number, and he answers right away.

"No, m'dear, Josie hasn't come back yet. Duncan has brought you up-to-date, I'm sure. Just sitting here pondering. The more we find out the less we know, it seems. I suppose we have to be patient until the body has been properly identified. Which could take a while, as the chief said. He seems to have no doubt that it's Brian. Unfortunately, it seems to be a reasonable assumption, under the circumstances."

Annie grips the receiver a little tighter.

"Judge, promise not to get mad," she says.

"Now Annie, why would I get mad?"

"Promise."

"I never make a promise I'm not sure I can keep," he says, already suspicious.

"Oh, well. Okay. I just thought of something. There might be an easy way to identify the body."

"Yes?"

Annie looks at Duncan, who is standing by the window with his back turned, listening intently.

"Brian's old dental records. I know someone who has a set."

There is silence at the other end of the line. Silence reigns in Duncan's office as well. Then, Duncan turns around at precisely the same time that Judge offers a few well-chosen words into Annie's ear. She holds the receiver at arm's length.

"You promised," she tries.

"I did not, as you well remember. Now, Annie, where in blazes are these records?"

"In Louisville, Tennessee. You see, I was trying to find a way to reach someone in Brian's family, and when I was at my dentist's making a new appointment and looking at all those records behind the receptionist, you know, it just occurred to me that maybe it wouldn't be too hard to find a dentist in a small town…"

"Yes, yes, I get the idea. And so you found his dentist?"

"Well, his dentist from way back before he left home. He told me Brian had left Louisville all those years ago to go into the service, and he hadn't seen him since. He figured somebody would call to have the records transferred at some point, but it never happened. So he still has them."

"He gave you this information over the phone?" Judge asks, sounding a bit dumbfounded.

"Not right away, only after I told him it was an emergency."

"An emergency. I see. And do you still have his number?"

"Yes, but it's at home. His name is Dr. Bromfield. I can get it for you; I'll just look him up again on the net."

"Good grief, girl, I don't know whether to kiss you or keel-haul you."

"Depends on what we find out, doesn't it? I'm not batting a thousand so far. Everything I find out just seems to put Jean deeper in trouble."

"That's the thing about truth, m'dear. You just always have to hope that you'll end up on the right side of it. I've found that out the hard way a few times, believe me. You get that dentist's number for me and I'll give him a call, and I'll have Josie call you when she gets back if she has any news on Jean."

Annie hangs up and looks dolefully at Duncan.

"Are *you* mad at me?" she asks.

"How can I be mad at you? A bit exasperated, I'll admit, but I'm learning to expect these things now. Do you have any more surprises? I think I'd rather know up front. The one thing I'm going to remind you of is that we made an agreement about making phone calls. You were going to wait until we agreed the time was right. Wasn't that how we left it?"

"Yes, but I was only looking for information; I wasn't going to *do* anything with it..."

"But now you have."

"Well, that way we'll know the truth, won't we? Like Judge said, you just have to hope you end up on the right side of it."

"I don't know about you. Sharp as a fox one minute, innocent, blithe Pollyanna the next. A regular Jekyll and Hyde. I'm not sure I have the intestinal fortitude to live with you."

Annie glares at him, frowning, trying to determine whether he's joking, but she can't read his face.

"I'll leave you to ponder that question," she says. "I've got a ton of work that needs my sharp brain before I go home and do my blithe housewife bit. Will we be walking home separately?" she asks, testing.

"Hm. Now, Annie, don't take this the wrong way, but I do have to show up at the Friends of the Library meeting for a little while. Gifford called me earlier. Mentioned that they've had some calls from people who ordinarily make donations around Christmas, but with all the scandals around the library this year, a few of these people are getting cold feet."

An evasive answer if she's ever heard one. How fortunate for him to have a legitimate excuse. Maybe it's just as well. Annie doesn't really feel up to a standoff. This getting married thing is turning out to be a lot tougher than she had thought, especially with the two of them being set in their ways and with one of them being the cause of one of those previous scandals surrounding the library. Oh, that dratted Ridley, could she be the one stirring up trouble with the Friends, too? Of course. That must be how it is.

"No doubt all those cold feet are Ridley's doing," Annie hisses.

"Now, Annie—"

"I know, I know. I'm going to shut up now. Don't forget we're going to Sally and Matt's for dinner. If you think you're going to be late, give me a call. I'm going out for a quick coffee with Clare, but I'll be back at my desk after that."

"You mean you intend to come back and put your sharp brain to use on *library matters?* Who will carry on with the sleuthing?"

That gets him a scathing glance, but Annie feels a stab of guilt as she hurries down the stairs, which intensifies as she takes a look at the stack of work piling up on her desk. She shrugs and buzzes Clare. "Ready whenever you are."

It's snowing now, and Annie pulls her coat tightly around her, disregarding the fact that it's still wet from her walk on the beach. The snow is building up on the sidewalks and on the sloping lawn of the Congregational Church. The windows in the coffee shop are all steamed up, which is a good sign. It will be warm in there. Clare has already taken a small table on the side, and Annie joins her. It feels just like the old days, and she nurses a hope that their old friendship can be recaptured.

"So, how's Pavarotti?" Annie asks. Pavarotti is Clare's cockatiel. This particular feathered creature likes to hang upside in his cage and croon like a lovesick tenor. Clare has a menagerie of stray pets, some rather unsavory characters among them, Annie thinks, but Pavarotti is special.

"Oh, the poor thing. He misses you, Annie. Nobody else wants to sing duets with him. He squawks every time somebody knocks on my door; I'm sure he's hoping it's you. You know *I* can't carry a tune," she says, laughing.

Annie had tried to teach Pavarotti to sing Verdi and Puccini, with questionable success, but the wanna-be tenor had screeched joyously every time he heard Annie's voice.

"I miss him, too. And I miss you, Clare," Annie says, willing to give the old friendship a chance. "What's happening with you? Still meeting with the old gang?"

"Sure, we get together every couple of weeks. They're all coming to my house next Friday. You're welcome! Diana will be there; she still asks for you."

"Really? Has she got her big novel published yet?"

"No. Actually, she just decided she's going to become a poet. She says it's okay to be a poet and be unpublished... nobody expects it."

"Sounds like Diana, all right. So, anybody new in your life?"

"Well...as usual with me, it's a long story. I don't know quite how to begin, but...hm...you remember that Stuart and I...eh, had, you know...um, were together for a while?"

"How can I forget? I still can't fathom how that happened."

"Before you say anything else, Annie, Stuart and I, well..." Clare looks around in the coffee shop to check for listeners, but the two librarians are almost alone. A couple of out-of-towners sit at the counter listening to the radio. It is broadcasting local news—as though another fender-bender on 128 is of earth-shaking importance. Annie stares at Clare.

"You don't mean to tell me that you and Stu...that you're *involved* again?" she asks quietly.

Clare nods, looking slightly guilty and embarrassed, but Annie perceives a certain dreamy look in her eyes. Time to tread carefully. She'd better let Clare do the talking.

"I know what you're thinking, but you don't know Stu, not really. All that stuff that you see, you know, that superior and sort of sarcastic shell, well, there's more to him than that. Trust me. Anyway, I wanted you to know about it from me, before somebody figures it out and you hear it somewhere else."

"Clare, there's a lot that passes my understanding lately. As long as you're going into it with your eyes open, good luck to you." Annie can't think of a more positive comment to make, and decides it's better to leave it at that. To hide an awkward silence, she gets busy with her pistachio muffin. "Mmm, just baked, I think. It's still warm."

"Nuked. Didn't you hear the beep? Next time, we should try some of those new pastries."

"Maybe. Listen, Clare, I promise to come over to do a duet with Pavarotti soon, and I might even take you up on the invite for next week, but I've got to get back to my desk. The boss is making some veiled comments about me neglecting my work lately."

"And *I* didn't get done with the Large Prints. Thanks for listening, Annie. This has been on my mind a lot lately. I know you probably don't understand, but..."

"As long as you're happy, kid." *Let's not get maudlin, here.*

They brave the wind coming in from the sea, the sharp sleet biting their faces. The wind is whipping up the sea, too. There is likely to be some serious coastal erosion before this storm is over. Annie thinks about the rocky sea wall on the harbor side of her house. Well, it's held for a couple of hundred years. Poor Gussie, though, all alone in that whistling, whining house. Gussie doesn't like storms. By now, he'll be whining right along with the wind.

"Listen, Clare, would you mind telling Duncan that I just went home to check on Gussie? Gussie hates storms; I just want to wrap him up in a blanket. That seems to calm him."

"Sure thing, Annie. Give him a noogie from me." A noogie is a special knuckle love-pat that Clare gives to dogs, just below the chin.

Annie hurries home and takes care of Gussie, giving him the noogie. It makes her think of Bella, wishing she could give *her* a noogie, too. If anyone needs a noogie, it's that poor girl. Annie rashly gathers up a bag of cookies and some fat slices of Nisu, and hops in the car. She drives back along the beaches and across Keystone Bridge, and continues deeper into the Cove.

Just past the Tool Company, she turns down onto Breakwater Avenue and drives up around the corner into the Pigeon Cove Circle parking lot. Pigeon Cove Circle is a small hall overlooking the wreck that is all that's left of the old Tool Company. The Circle is run by a group of women who rent it out for parties and events. Annie's mother, Mairead, had been a member of the group while the family still lived in Pigeon Cove, and Annie remembers helping with the clean-up after parties now and then. The hall is also the Pigeon Covers' voting place, and, when not in use, the main room is chock-a-block with tables and folding chairs and voting booths, along with an old piano. Not to forget a couple of upholstered chairs, usually claimed by officials who come inspect the voting and make sure all rules are followed.

"Hello, old Mustard Palace," she says, parking her car facing the Tool Company. It's her nickname for the place ever since they sprayed that yellowy brown stuff on the walls, supposedly to keep the building from polluting the environment as it deteriorated. It looks ghastly. She steps out of the car and walks down to the back of the building. Annie still feels shocked every time she sees what has happened to the place since her dad worked there. It had started as the Pigeon Cove Smithy in the 1850's and became the Cape Ann Tool Company in 1891. When curious people come to the reference desk and ask Annie what was produced at the forge, she tells them that the most famous items forged there were probably the parts made for the Wright Whirlwind Engine in the "Spirit of St. Louis," which took Charles Lindberg on his pioneer crossing of the Atlantic. The company also produced vast amounts of materials during both world wars, with the workers on a twenty-four-hour schedule. While the neighbors in those days sometimes complained about the sound of hammers banging around the clock, all recognized the importance of the contribution to the front during the war. When peace arrived, the company turned to producing forgings for various peaceful industrial needs, from oil wells to sewing machines. Those were the years her father had worked there.

Annie stands outside the building for a moment with her eyes closed, her hand on the corrugated siding. She still remembers the way it was when she lived in the Cove. The sounds from the forge: the pounding of the hammers, the rushing noise of the blasting furnaces, the workers shouting to make themselves heard over the thunderous din and clang. She remembers the way it looked when those great iron doors were open and you could look inside and see the furnaces blazing. She would look around, trying to catch sight of her dad, and when she caught his eye she would wave, and sometimes he would be able to come out and see her. Black and grimy, he had been, like a chimneysweep.

Oh, but now, look at it. The corrugated siding of the building is torn and flapping in the wind; trees are growing in the vast expanse inside, and here and there the harbor is visible between cracks in the walls. Once, long ago, a flock of pigeons had been washed ashore in this cove during a great storm, giving the name to this section of town. As much as she will miss the Tool Company when it's gone, she is looking forward to the day when it is torn down to make room for whatever will replace it. Plans have been offered for a motel; a restaurant; condo apartments with a park or recreational harbor; or a combination of uses, but the old wreck still stands, along with the tall, white-painted chimneystack that is sometimes mistaken for a lighthouse by boaters out at sea.

Annie knows a way to get in. After the forge closed she used to sneak in now and then, just to walk around and remember the old place. However, today it's pitch dark inside, and she hadn't thought to bring a flashlight. She stumbles along through heaps of metal scrap and boxes of trash. Apparently, some people have found yet another way to get rid of stuff without paying at the transfer station.

"Bella!" she calls softly. There's no answer. Annie waddles through a wet and sloppy area, losing a sense of where she is in the darkness. Suddenly, the floor seems to vanish beneath her feet. She manages at the last moment to grab hold of something solid, which turns out to be the rusty anvil sitting atop one of the drop forges her father had worked on. Her right leg is hanging over the edge of a water-filled hole, and she carefully pulls herself back up, hoping the forge is still anchored to the floor. Once upright, she takes a deep breath without moving a muscle. "Thanks, Dad," she whispers, giving the anvil a pat.

As she gets used to the dark, the surroundings become more visible. She has almost fallen into a jagged opening in the floor. How could Bella find a place to sleep here? The whole place is falling apart, with the help of water pouring in from above and waves sloshing up from below. The old forge was built out over the bay of Pigeon Cove Harbor, and the floor is giving way. Right now, with the tide coming in, the ocean is welling up through holes all over the floor, including the one she nearly fell into. Among the trash and broken down machinery, she notices something else. Annie covers her mouth to stifle a cry. She pulls herself together and makes her way over to a limp body. She grabs at the clothing, which only serves to partially undress the body. Finally the gets a firm hold of a stiff and cold hand, and tries to pull the lifeless human being away from the edge of a water hole. A large wave surges in and helps her along. Before it recedes, she manages to pull the body over to where it can't get sucked down by another wave. Annie bends down for a closer look—close enough, even in the darkness, to determine that the human being is Bella. She looks in a daze at the pale, grimy face before leaving the body trapped behind a solid structure in a corner, and then she stumbles off into a dry section of the forge. She hears a rattling noise somewhere else in the building, and panics. Standing stock still, she finally decides it must be the wind causing the corrugated siding to flap and rattle. After taking a deep breath, she feels in her pocket for the cell phone, but she left it in her desk drawer at the library. Instead, she finds her way to the outside, and runs up toward the Pigeon Cove Circle. She knocks on a window. While waiting, she looks back down toward the forge. She imagines seeing a shadow through one of the grimy windows. Just then, an elderly woman opens the door.

"Oh, hi, Annie, what's up? Haven't seen you for a long time."

Annie recognizes Edna, who had been there back in Mairead's day, but Annie can't even take time for a civilized hello.

"Oh, Edna, may I use your phone to call the police? There's been an accident..."

"Oh...sure, Annie, come on in," Edna says, backing away and pointing to the phone.

"Chief Murphy, this is Annie Quitnot. I've found Bella."

When she finishes telling him where she is, she hangs up and calls Duncan, who tells her to wait in the hall until he gets there.

"Stay there. Promise. Don't move."

• • •

Chief Murphy arrives first, sirens blaring. Annie stays inside. She doesn't really want the chief to see her before Duncan gets there, but the chief drives right up to the hall and walks in, nodding to Edna when she lets him by.

"So, Ms. Quitnot, where is Bella?"

Annie opens her mouth before shaking her head a little, and points to the Tool Company.

"Bella's in there...dead...she's dead, Chief. I pulled her away from a hole, away from the water. I can't go back in there again...you'll find her..."

"Stay here. Don't leave." He gestures to Officer Elwell to wait outside.

"My husband's on the way, I'm waiting for him. There he is," she says, as Duncan's Cooper comes speeding around the corner onto Breakwater Avenue.

Chief Murphy hurries outside. Billy Hale gets out of the cruiser and joins the chief, followed by other arriving officers, and they enter the Tool Company, the chief motioning to Elwell to come down and stand outside.

Duncan gives Annie a silent hug.

"Oh, Dunc. I just drove over to bring her something to eat. Esa told me this is where she's been staying..."

"It's all right, Annie. Don't cry, love." Which really sets her off on a crying jag. More sirens are heard, and the ambulance arrives.

"They won't need an ambulance," Annie says.

"Well, it's required, I guess."

Duncan starts to walk down there, but Elwell just tells him to go back up and stay in the hall and wait for word from the chief. After a few minutes, Chief Murphy appears. He signals to the ambulance driver to wait and walks up toward the hall. Annie and Duncan go outside and join the chief on the sidewalk.

"Ms. Quitnot, what on earth made you come here?"

Annie explains, and the chief just shakes his head.

"Well, go home now, please. There is nothing more you can do. We are taking care of her. I will want to talk to you later, though." He nods to Duncan and turns to go back down to the forge.

"Chief Murphy," Annie says, a little hesitantly, "do you think it's possible now that Bella could have been a witness?"

"I don't know, Ms. Quitnot. But, please, you've just had a shock and need to calm down. Mr. Langmuir, take your wife home and keep her out of any more trouble."

Duncan nods and grabs Annie by the hand. "Come on, Annie, let's go. Want to ride home in my car?"

"Thanks, I'll be okay now. I'll drive my car and meet you there."

"Don't make any stops on the way, now, promise me?" Duncan opens the door for her.

Annie blows her nose and starts the engine. *As if things could get any worse,* she thinks. Duncan opens her door again and leans in. "Remember, we are going over to Sally and Matt's for dinner," he says, hoping that this will help bring her around. And it does, as Annie almost smiles. He stands with one hand on the roof of her car, not letting her leave. Annie looks at him and holds up a hand to stop him from speaking.

"Duncan, I know what you'd like to say: we can't mention this tonight. I agree. In fact, I need to not even think about it tonight. I'll think about it tomorrow. But I do have to find out how this happened to Bella, you know that."

"And if it's connected to Jean. Yes, I know that. Let the police work on it first. Maybe there's a reasonable explanation. Maybe it was even an accident," he suggests hopefully.

"Now who's Pollyanna?" she asks, shaking her head.

Rather than go back down to Breakwater Avenue and drive past the Tool Company, Annie takes a left up the hill and goes around the block back to Granite Street. When she passes the front of the forge, she notices several cars parked alongside, engines running. Gawkers, ambulance chasers, and maybe a local reporter.

CHAPTER TWENTY-FIVE

"Our two souls therefore which are one,
Though I must go, endure not yet
A breach, but an expansion,
Like gold to airy thinness beat."
(John Donne, "A Valediction Forbidding Mourning")

Jean dreams.

"What?"

"You heard me, Jeanie, I've joined the Navy. I must make my way somehow. We both have to get out of this place, don't we? Staying here will kill us. You know that. Joining the Navy is the only way I could think of. Even if it's just for a few years, and who knows, it might turn into a career?"

Jean moans, her lips part a fraction, her fingers move on the blanket, tentacle-like, *open, close, open, close.* She quiets down and lies perfectly still.

Josie leans forward and takes Jean's hand, which is cold and dry. There is no response; the poor woman simply lies there as though petrified, fingers stiff, arms rigid. Josie pats Jean's hand and rubs her arm a little, trying to smooth the tenseness out of it. She wonders if the hospital has started some sort of physical therapy yet. She knows that if they have not, Jean's whole body will soon begin to stiffen.

"There, there, Jean, everything's going to be all right, you'll see," she whispers.

The guard steps closer, no doubt in order to hear more of the conversation.

Josie gives him a stinging look. She would like to talk to Jean, thinking this is probably what the woman needs the most, someone to penetrate the thick fog that surrounds her. Talk about her husband, jog her mind in order to wake her up, but she feels awkward with the guard there. She pats Jean's inflexible hand reassuringly and continues rubbing her arms and legs. Slowly, Jean's whole body seems to soften and her muscles lose their tenseness. Then she drops back down into that dark, warm place where nobody can reach her, the only place where she feels safe.

She's a little nervous, talking to the elderly woman. They are sitting in the woman's living room, on a couch that is covered with a fringed blanket. On the walls are religious images: a picture of Jesus, a small wooden cross, and some colorfully embroidered Bible quotes. A row of healthy African violets lines the windowsill.

"I'm waiting for my husband to come back, Mrs. Bellingham. He's in Grenada right now." A little shyly, she holds out her hand, showing off the small, glittering stone and a narrow gold band.

"Are you living with your family, then?"

"No, I've been staying with friends until I find a place of my own. My husband's in the Navy, you see; he joined last year. I might get to see him at Christmas. I don't have any other family." She blushes a little, lying like that, but the woman doesn't seem to notice.

"Dear, dear, you poor little thing...he is in the invasion? I'm sure he will come home safe. And Christmas is only two months away."

"Yes...only I'll probably have to go down to Virginia to see him; otherwise, we won't have much time together."

"My goodness. Are you working yourself, also?"

"Certainly. I work in a pharmacy on Fifth Street."

"Oh, yes, I know that one. Well, that's quite near, isn't it? Then I think everything's in order, dear. I guess you've just found your place. We'd love to have you, as long as you understand that we like it nice and quiet. No pets, no late night parties, like that."

"Of course. Oh, thank you so much. When can I move in?"

"Tomorrow, if you like. Do you have much furniture?"

"Oh, no. You see, my husband left right after the wedding, so I don't have any furniture at all. I'll have to buy what I need. I've just been renting a room."

"I see." The woman looks at her carefully, as if to size her up. "You know, we may have a couple of old things in the attic that you could borrow until you get your own, a bed, maybe, and some chairs."

"That is very nice of you, Mrs. Bellingham, thank you. I promise to take good care of everything and to return the things as soon as I can afford to get my own."

*She leaves the house on Myrtle Avenue feeling free and grownup. She's finally on her own, in faraway Laurel, Maryland, out from under Mama's eagle eyes. She hasn't even told Mama where she is, only called the family lawyer before she left Louisville. Mr. Bentley knows everything about their family, including Papa not being her real father. When she was little, she used to call Mr. Bentley "Uncle Paul," but he isn't really related. He had been happy for her though, had sounded proud even, when she told him she was moving away from home, away from Louisville. Once she has a telephone installed, she will call and give him her number in case of emergency.*_

Josie can sense the change in Jean. The hands feel warmer; the joints are not so rigid. She even looks younger, with that slight blush in her cheek. Josie takes hold of the dormant hand again and pats it encouragingly.

"That's my girl. Just hang in there, Jean. Get your rest. Maybe tomorrow you can wake up. Don't rush it. Just rest. I'll be going now, but I'll come back tomorrow." She lets go of Jean's hand and turns to look at the guard.

"I guess I'll go now, but I'll be back again."

"Better make sure you have permission first."

"Don't worry. What are you afraid of anyway? Do you think I would try to sneak this poor, unconscious woman out of here?"

"I've got my orders, that's all. She could be faking it for all I know. Happens all the time."

CHAPTER TWENTY-SIX

"Serenely full, the epicure would say,
Fate cannot harm me, I have dined today."
(Sydney Smith, Lady Holland's Memoir)

Annie wraps the Zinfandel in purple tissue, which she twists around the neck of the bottle. She fluffs the top of the tissue into a flower and ties a bow with a piece of fancy ribbon from her scrap-wrap-bag, which contains generations of used wrapping materials that were just too good to throw away. Annie's a pack rat when it comes to certain things—tiny boxes; candle ends that she plans to melt down to dip new candles; treasured old fountain pens that may one day be restored. After curling the ribbon to take the kinks out of it, she sticks the bottle back into the refrigerator until it's time to go.

• • •

Despite her promise to Duncan and the chief to stick around the house, Annie decides that a short ride will help calm her nerves. She drives back to Pigeon Cove, parks on Granite Pier, and then takes the trail that goes under Keystone Bridge and continues along Flat Ledge Quarry. From below, the bridge looms immense, and under the arch a trail leads from the bright light of Sandy Bay through a peculiar, echoing darkness to the other side. It always has a mysterious, otherworldly effect on Annie, bringing her back to another time, when she walked here with her parents. Over on the right, the water in the quarry reflects the granite wall looming on the other side.

Looking back at the massive arch of the bridge, she studies the great rocky cleft underneath it. Her dad once told her how quarry workers had tunneled through the granite to connect two quarries and create a downhill railroad bed, to make it easier to deliver granite to the pier. He also said that some local newspaper reporter at the time had written about the *gravitation road,* suggesting that the cars and their loads would hurtle into the sea—which came true more than once, when both cars and their loads were dumped beyond the pier. Annie still remembers a couple of the names of the quarry locomotives: Polyphemus and Vulcan.

She ambles back to the car and drives up Landmark Lane, parks the car and goes for a quick walk in the woods. The air is chilly, and the pines whine in the wind. When she realizes she has taken a path toward Steel Derrick, she shudders and turns around. Half an hour later, she's back at the car. The Chevy balks a little at having to start in the cold, but soon hits the steep downhill and speeds up. In fact…it starts going too fast. Annie presses harder on the break, but to no avail. She begins to panic. The road goes straight down, and at this speed, she'd never be able to make a turn into one of the driveways. *Oh no, am I going to hurtle into the sea?* she has time to think. At the bottom of the lane she has a split-second choice: hard left, hard right or straight across into a stone wall. She opts for hard left, and the car does a one-eighty before coming to a screeching halt, tires smoking, facing the traffic. After swallowing hard, Annie gets out of the car and sits down on the stone wall until she can breathe normally.

Fortunately, there is a repair shop nearby and she walks over, albeit on shaky legs, and talks to the crew. They agree to go and get the car, and Annie calls Duncan. While on the phone, she hears sirens in the distance. Someone has called to report the accident. A few minutes later Duncan pulls up, looking relieved to find her in one piece. Annie has to confess to breaking her promise, and Duncan, paling a bit as she describes what happened, simply shakes his head. He keeps a tight grip on her hand until she is safely installed in his car. They sit mute during the short ride home, Duncan focusing on driving.

"They said I might be without a car for a day or two...so, we're a one-car family again, now...at least temporarily. If you can call this little toy a car..." Annie says, trying to lighten the mood as they near home.

Duncan makes a face as he pulls into the driveway and Annie laughs, remembering the first time she'd seen Duncan get out of his new mini-Cooper. Annie's eyebrows had nearly merged with her hairline then, and she'd had to contain herself from making a derogatory comment. That had been before they were married, of course.

"So? I forgot to ask...have the Friends deserted us yet?" Sitting in front of the mirror in their bedroom she puts the hair brush down and dabs on some lipstick.

"Unfortunately, some of them have, yes. Or at least they have deferred making donations until the current *'situation'* has been resolved. They are very apologetic, *'Oh, Mr. Langmuir, you understand why we hesitate...'* and, of course, I do have to be polite and understanding. By the way, you look...um...different. Do I have to dress up, too? If you are Sacagawea, who am I supposed to be?" he says, eyeing Annie's ankle-length cotton shift.

"Whatever you're wearing, make sure it's machine washable. Lobster tonight..." she says. She decides to hold back on any snide comments about library patrons' lack of faith and loyalty.

Ben and Brad, Sally's twins, fight about who is to open the door and let the guests in. Brad is the one with the smug smile this time, and Ben slips away, moping.

"Come in! Sit yourselves down! These monsters of the deep will get tough if we don't dig right in."

Matt carries the platter heaped with steaming lobsters, two per person and a few extra for good measure, and Sally follows with the individual pots of butter and lemon wedges. Ben brings bread and salad to the table, and Matt undoes the foil to uncork the wine. Underneath the foil there is a screw top. He checks the label, raises his eyebrows, and looks at Duncan.

"I've got some beer in the cooler," he offers, with a deadpan look.

Duncan produces a sort of silly smile and nods. Sally and Annie don't mind. All the more for them. Just because Annie would prefer Rockport to remain a dry town doesn't mean she doesn't enjoy a glass of wine or two. Well, the referendum will be coming up again soon.

They dig in. Duncan manages tails and claws fine, but that's as far as he goes. As usual, Annie charitably helps him with the rest. They are lounging around the table in the aftermath of gorging themselves, dipping crusty bread into the remaining lobster butter and sucking at stray legs, when the doorbell rings. Ben beats Brad this time. Sally brings Tim into the kitchen. He is wearing pajamas and has a blanket draped around his shoulders Indian chief style. Sally shakes the snow off the blanket and goes to get him a dry one. Tim looks pale and is unusually quiet. After a few moments, Sally returns.

"Well, boys, off you go. You can watch TV in the den. I'll make up a bed for Tim as soon as we're finished with dinner."

When the noise of the TV can be heard, Sally looks at Matt.

"It was Lorraine who brought Tim over. Poor thing, she was crying. Jack's drunk again, going after Tim and giving him a hard time, she said, so she wanted the boy out of the house. Guess Jack was getting a bit violent again." Sally avoids looking at Annie, knowing how she feels about Lorraine, but Annie surprises her.

"Good idea to send Tim away. Does this happen a lot?"

"Often enough. Tim spends a good deal of time with us. He's not as tough as you may think. He just acts that way."

"I can understand why. Is Tim getting any help? Counseling, I mean."

"Lorraine doesn't want people to know about Jack's problem. She thinks she can handle it herself. Anyway, friends, I'm planning on having a good time tonight. Coffee's on. Want yours Irish style, Annie? You guys can take care of yourselves. Let's move into the living room and change the subject."

Which they do.

• • •

Annie wakes up in the middle of the night. She tosses and turns for a while, trying to go back to sleep, but there's no fighting nature. *Too much wine, and then all that coffee.* She groans. Sally and she had started discussing Jean, of course, and had finished the bottle of Zinfandel between them and then moved on to Irish coffee without missing a beat. *Oh, isn't hindsight wonderful.* Her ears are ringing; it sounds like a field of crickets has invaded the bedroom. Shellfish and wine and olives, a perfect recipe for a migraine. *Oh, hopefully not.*

She tries to think of something else in order to go back to sleep, and remembers that at one point in their conversation last night, Sally and she had discussed Annie's phone call to Brian's brother, Mitchell. That phone call is bothering Annie right now. It was something Mitchell had said, but what was it? "Brian left *heah yeahs ago. Went into the sehvice. Moved to Virginny.*" That's it, *Virginia.* What if that is where he has been going when he leaves Rockport? What if that is where he works, where he has a home away from home? What if that is *not* his body in the morgue? What if Virginia is where Brian is now, maybe unaware of what has happened to Jean? Or, going back to her earlier suspicion, maybe that's where he leads a secret second life, which Jean may have figured out?

There's no help for it now; sleep will not come. Annie sneaks out of the bedroom and grabs Duncan's robe. Downstairs, there's still some coffee in the pot, and she pours some into a mug and zaps it. She turns on some Renaissance music, a favorite album with the King's Singers, keeping the volume low even though she normally loves to listen to it at cathedral volume, and turns on the computer.

The computer is humming reassuringly, the screensaver playing its endless slide show of famous Hamlets, Ophelias, Romeos, Juliets, Othellos and other Shakespearean characters. Barrymore, Olivier, Ashcroft, Dench, Burton, Gielgud, the Redgraves, Jacobi, Branagh: a parade of the best. Annie kisses her finger and touches the desktop image of Droeshut's engraved portrait of Shakespeare, right on the bard's seductive lips. She lets her eyes glide lovingly over the spade-shaped collar, the embroidered garment covering that great heart, the tall brow that is shaped in a mirror image of the chin, the wavy hair, the long nose with its sensuously flared nostrils, the curiously curled mustache. At the last, she looks into his eyes, those deep, elusive pools of wisdom.

"Hi, Willie, sorry to wake you. I know it's three o'clock in the morning, but I can't sleep. Help me out here. You know a lot about love and deception, truth and falsehood, not to mention fools and impostors."

She gets on the Internet, tries "Stokes" and "Virginia." Keep it simple, wide-open, not too many delimiters to start with.

Nope, too many hits. Maybe *Norfolk,* if Brian's job is still in connection with the Navy? She types in "Stokes" and "Norfolk VA." Better. Just a few. She clicks on a likely hit, finds a phone listing for a B. Stokes, and jots the information down. As she scrolls, quickly scanning each hit, she runs across an obituary. She opens it and reads it. Reads it again.

"It can't be," she says. But she knows it must be, and prints it out.

"Rebecca Louise Stokes, 39, died Feb. 20, after a long and courageous fight with illness, surrounded by her loving family. She leaves her husband, Brian Stokes, formerly of Louisville, Tennessee, and their children, William, 10, and Louisa, 7. Rebecca loved her family and was an avid gardener. She was a volunteer at the Union Elementary School and at St. Elizabeth's Nursing Home. The family asks that Rebecca will be remembered with memorial contributions to the United Methodist Church and the Norfolk Garden Club."

Brian is a bigamist. That's why he hasn't showed up. Is he a killer, too? Did Rebecca Louise leave anything behind besides her children? Something worth a little effort to help speed her on her way? And then, having succeeded, had he tried again with Jean? The house is in Jean's name, but surely there must be a will. And, as Mrs. Ridley says, their house is "worth a mint." Maybe Brian has someone else waiting in the wings, someone young and pretty and demanding.

CHAPTER TWENTY-SEVEN

"Other sins only speak; murder shrieks out."
(John Webster, Duchess of Malfi)

Annie turns off the King's Singers, whose voices are weaving a glorious rendition of "Sing Joyfully," which now instead clashes painfully with her mood. At four o'clock, the alarm horn blares at the fire station. She counts the honks, one, two, three. Ambulance call. The ambulance squeals by, going up Cove Hill toward the South End. Annie looks out the window. The trees are heavy with snow, as are the streets, softening the noise of vehicles. Police cruisers follow, blue lights flashing, sirens screaming, even in the night. Must be serious. Of course, the South End is an affluent part of town, and a little extra efficiency there won't go amiss. In the silence that follows, she knows it's too late to go back to bed; she'll hardly have time to fall asleep before she has to wake up again. She starts a fresh pot of coffee, and then the phone rings. It's Sally, who is crying.

"Sally, calm down, I can't hear a word you're saying. Try speaking only one word at a time, and take a breath in between. Now, concentrate."

"Davis' house...shots... sob...police..." Sally breaks down again.

"Sally, are they dead?" Annie asks carefully.

"I don't...sob...know...oh, Annie..."

"Where's Matt?" Annie asks, suddenly worried that Matt may have ventured outside to check things out.

"With the boys..." she stops to whimper, "...and the police..."

"Oh yes, Tim! He's still with you?"

Now Sally is coming apart and starts sobbing hysterically, unable to get another word out.

"I'll be right there, Sal." Annie hangs up and runs upstairs. Duncan is wide awake, sitting on the edge of the bed.

"What on earth is going on? Is there a fire? Who called?"

Annie tells him what she knows while she throws her clothes on. Duncan gets dressed, too. If she's going over there, so is he. Especially since, as she had pointed out earlier, they are a one-car family now. As they pull out of the driveway, sliding on the deepening snow, Annie notices lights on in the neighborhood. The scanners are on, too, of course. People will be listening, trying to interpret the code words.

When they get to Eden Road, there's traffic. Judging by the tire marks in the snow, the gawkers are out already. Duncan drives past a couple of flashing police cruisers parked outside Lorraine's house and pulls into Sally's driveway. No sign of an ambulance; it must have left already. Chief Murphy, standing in Lorraine's doorway talking to Officer Elwell, catches Annie's eye as she gets out of the car. He looks grim.

Sally has calmed down somewhat and is making coffee. It's going to be a coffee kind of morning. Tim is sitting at the kitchen table, still in his pajamas, the blanket he came with now dry and pulled tightly around his shoulders. He looks even paler than last night, but he hasn't been crying. His eyes are wide and hard. In a state of shock, Annie assumes. Sally is trying to make him eat, pressing him to have some toast and hot cocoa. Matt shakes his head.

"Leave the boy alone, Sal. He'll have something in a while. All right, Tim?"

Tim stares at Matt and shudders involuntarily. Annie and Duncan join Tim at the table, and Ben and Brad appear, all dressed for school.

"Oh, I don't know if you boys should go to school today." Sally looks anxiously at them.

"Better to let them go," Matt says, and gets up and walks them out into the hall, cautioning them not to talk to their friends about anything they've seen or heard. There will be enough rumors. They nod.

Matt returns and puts a hand on Tim's shoulder.

"Come on, Tim. Time to get into some clothes. Let's go see what we can find. I'm sure we've got something that'll fit you; you're about Brad's size, aren't you?" Tim slides off the chair and follows Matt obediently, like a dog. When they are out of hearing range, Annie looks at Sally.

"Poor Tim. Will you keep him here with you today?"

"Of course. Unless someone comes to pick him up. They always cart the kids off, don't they? Stick them in a temporary foster home or something."

"But we don't know anything for sure about Jack and Lorraine yet…or do we?"

"No. Matt went over there when the police arrived, but they sent him right back. He did manage to tell Chief Murphy that we have Tim here. I suppose they'll come knocking on our door at any moment."

"Do you feel like telling us what happened? I mean, what you know," Duncan says.

"We woke up when we heard the shots. Boy, it's loud when it's right next door. And a scream. Lorraine's. Then silence. We jumped out of bed, thinking the worst. Matt was going to run right over there, but I wouldn't let him. I was afraid he'd get shot, too. I called the police, and they said they'd already had a call and were on their way. I could tell by Tim's face that he was afraid. The poor kid must have had some idea of what was going on. He just sank down into that chair in the kitchen, and never moved." Tears stream down Sally's cheeks.

"Matt's very good with Tim," Annie says, putting a hand on Sally's arm.

"I know," Sally says, looking over her shoulder to see whether Matt's still off with Tim, then speaks softly. "You know how rough it was for a while, when our own boys were fighting all the time. Matt and I fought, too, which only made it worse. I was overprotective, and he had to make up for it by being overly strict. I was very unfair. But we've got it pretty much worked out." She calms down, and smiles at Annie. "I have to admit that Matt's a great dad, and I try to agree with him now, even when I think he's being too strict. I'm always tempted to be more lenient. I'm such a softie."

They finish their coffee, and Annie helps clean up. Duncan looks out the window. The view of Twin Lights is as lovely as ever, the pre-dawn glow warming the color of the sky to a pale gold. Thacher Island lies snow covered, and the morning air is so cold that the sea is sending up great swaths and wisps of sea smoke. The snow reflects the brilliant light onto the sea smoke, creating a shimmering aura around the island. Nearer by, the Babson's lawn, with its few trees stunted by ocean winds, and the ledges and crags across the way leading down to the sea, look like a wintry picture postcard, but the flashing blue lights off to the right mar the vision. There is a knock on the door.

"Here it comes," Sally says.

Chief Murphy steps in and shakes the snow off his cap. A slightly orange tinge of day-old stubble adorns the jaw. He drags a hand across his hair, which doesn't do much to tame the carrot-colored frizz.

"I'd like to ask you and your husband a few questions...if you don't mind." He turns and looks somewhat pointedly at Annie and Duncan.

Duncan rises. "We'll be leaving, Chief. Just came to help out."

"Of course, Mr. Langmuir. What are friends for," the chief says hastily.

"Call me if you need me," Annie whispers as she leaves, "I'll be glad to stay with Tim if you both have to go somewhere."

CHAPTER TWENTY-EIGHT

"The meek, the terrible meek, the fierce agonizing meek,
Are about to enter into their inheritance."
(Charles Rann Kennedy, "The Terrible Meek")

Jean dreams.

"Hi, Uncle Paul," she says with a giggle.

"Jean, my favorite niece, is that you?"

"Yes, Mr. Bentley, it's me! I'm just calling to give you my telephone number. You see, I'm living in my own apartment now, and I have my own phone! I have a job, too, at a pharmacy nearby..."

"Jean...Jeanie, my girl, I am very sorry, but I must interrupt you. I have tried to reach you, but I had no number, no address, even..."

"What is it, Mr. Bentley? You sound so serious."

"It is serious, my girl. Your mama, well, your mama..." Bentley hesitates, and Jean knows.

"She's dead, isn't she?"

"Yes, Jean, she's dead. And buried, I'm afraid."

She is almost relieved to hear it. Not relieved that her mama is dead, that would be...well, shameful and immoral, but relieved that she doesn't have to go to the funeral and pretend. Oh, but even thinking it is disrespectful too.

"Oh," she says, simply. What else can she say?

"My condolences, of course, dear," he says, although Mr. Bentley knows full well that she and her mama had not parted on the best of terms. "And now, Jean, we have the will to deal with."

Well, now, that won't concern her much. Mama wouldn't have left her anything. Mama had always despised that illegitimate child of hers. A daughter born too soon after the wedding, a child who had forever after reminded her of a foolish mistake, falling for that fly-by-night man with the violet eyes, the man who had made her pregnant and then deserted her. The mere sight of this daughter had rankled and given Mama those powerful migraines. Whatever Mama left behind in the world would all go to some goody-goody charity, or to the church, of this she was sure.

"You see, it's all in your name, Jean. You are the sole beneficiary. You're not rich, of course, but there's enough there to give you a bit of a start. But, first, you need to come here so we can talk about it."

She feels a little sick to her stomach. Mama had actually left her everything? No, she knows with unshakable certainty that it must have been Papa's doing. He was the one who had taken care of the money, the bills, the insurance, and, certainly, the will. Oh, maybe Mama had signed something, but she had probably had enough Southern Comfort in her at the time that she would have signed away her own left foot. But now, to go back home?

"Oh, no, Mr. Bentley. I can't go back there, no, no."

"But the house, Jean, it's yours, now. Yours to live in, with no one else in it."

"Never. I will never, ever live there. I will sell it. Will you help me with that, Mr. Bentley?"

"Oh, dear. Yes, of course, Jean, if that's what you really want. But, first, I'd like to talk to you in person. If I wire you some money, which you can pay me back as soon as the estate is settled, will you come and meet me in Knoxville, if you don't want to come to Louisville?"

"Of course, if I must. But I would have to ask permission from the pharmacy to take the time off."

"You do that, Jean, and then you call me back. Let's try to meet next week, say on Tuesday? I have all of Tuesday free."

"Okay, Mr. Bentley. I just hope they don't get mad at me at the pharmacy."

Dr. Kim studies his patient. He has noticed small changes in her and hopes they are signs that she is returning to consciousness. Her arms are not quite so rigid. The face has a different sheen to it, a suppleness that looks healthier than the taut, almost cadaver-like appearance he had noted only yesterday. *Well, time will tell.*

CHAPTER TWENTY-NINE

"Without a grave, unknelled, uncoffin'd,
and unknown."
(Lord Byron, "Childe Harold's Pilgrimage")

"Annie, can you come up to my office?" There is a note in Duncan's voice that she can't interpret. It must be about Jack and Lorraine. She excuses herself to a patron who is looking in the vertical file for some information on the history of the Rockport Granite Industry.

"I'll be back down in a few minutes. If the information you need isn't in that file, we can go down to the Local History Room to look for it. We have a big display case down there on the granite industry."

The patron nods.

"Thank you, but I think I just found what I need in your map drawer. This map showing the quarries, may I copy it?"

"Yes, you may, just ask for the copier key over in circulation. And then if you would please put the map on my desk afterwards. I'll put it back in the map case." That way it won't be misfiled, never to be found again.

Annie takes the stairs two steps at a time and arrives breathless at Duncan's door.

"What is it, Dunc?"

"The body. *It isn't Brian,* Annie. The chief just called to tell Judge, and Judge called me. They got the set of x-rays from your Dr. Bromfield, and they don't match. At all, in fact. Brian Stokes apparently had one of his wisdom teeth pulled as a teenager, and the body has all his. That's pretty conclusive, I guess."

"Hah! I knew it!" Annie lets out enough breath to set the papers on Duncan's desk flying. "Sorry, Dunc. But then, who is it? Do they know?"

"Apparently not. Somebody from out-of-town, maybe. Nobody's been reported missing in town, and it's been a while."

"Maybe Mrs. Ridley has another brilliant idea?"

"Now, Annie, don't gloat. That'll just put you in her class."

"I guess you're right." Annie looks contrite. "Oh, did Judge say anything about Jack and Lorraine? I was sure that's what you were going to tell me about."

"Jack's dead. Lorraine is being operated on. Judge's guess is that Jack shot her and then himself, but that's not certain, and the police have officially put a cap on any news so far. Hopefully that's how it was; I'd sure hate to see it the other way around."

Annie sits back in her chair, shocked.

"Good Lord. Poor Tim. Whichever way it happened, what an awful memory that would be for a child to live with. I mean... either way, one of his parents is a murderer. Of course, I'm assuming it's Jack...and I sure hope Lorraine pulls through."

"Do I detect a slight note of charity here?"

"I learned a lot about Lorraine last night, Dunc. I admit it; I haven't been very charitable up until now. I hope I'll have a chance to make amends. Shows you how little we know about other people, sometimes."

"I'm beginning to have hopes for you, dear."

"Dear?"

Duncan covers his phone with both hands, as if somebody might be listening, and whispers, "Darling."

"The microphone is underneath the desk drawer, silly." Annie laughs because she needs to laugh. It sounds a little shrill.

"Oh, but Duncan, the news about the body not being Brian's...that's so strange..."

"I thought you'd be relieved?"

"I am, but I found something else...I don't know what it all means, now...I'm getting very confused." Annie pulls a paper out of her jacket pocket and hands it to him. He unfolds it and reads it. Then he reads it again, just as she had.

CHAPTER THIRTY

"To live a life half dead, a living death."
(John Milton, "Paradise Regained")

Jean dreams.

"Well, Jean, what do you think now? What will you do with the money?" Mr. Bentley sits behind the massive oak desk in his office.

"Buy a house up in New England," she says, looking quite determined. Her home in Louisville has been sold, along with most of the furniture. She has kept only a few things, mostly things that remind her of Papa. Mr. Bentley told her that she would not be rich, but, in her mind, she is wealthy. There hadn't been a lot of actual money left. Mama had used it all up "to live on" after Papa's death, but there's enough from the sale of the house to buy a modest place, far away from Louisville, with some money left over. A house just big enough to raise a family. And a car. Yes, that's it. That's how she will use the money.

"I'm going to buy a car and drive up to Cape Ann. Then we'll see."

Mr. Bentley shakes his head, looking concerned. "Be careful, girl; it's easy to use up the money. Be sure that you know what you want. Spend some time thinking about this. You'll have a family someday. Would that be where you'd want to bring up your children? What if you got homesick for Tennessee and wanted to move back here? It can be hard for children to be uprooted. It happened to me. It was painful losing my childhood friends. Well, whatever you decide, child, I'll help you. Your money is safe in the bank for now, but you'd be wise to invest it. I know someone who could help you there."

"My mind's made up, Uncle Paul. Tomorrow, I'm buying a car."

Josie sits by Jean's bedside. Jean's eyelashes are fluttering a little.

"Jean, wake up." Josie has been speaking softly to her, trying to engage the mind that she senses is still awake inside that sleeping body. "Jean, where's Brian? We've been trying to reach him. Can you tell us where he is, Jean?"

Jean's chest rises and sinks faster. Her eyelids tremble and open just the tiniest crack.

"Brian…" It is only a hoarse whisper, but Josie hears it, sees the lips forming the name.

"Yes, Jean, Brian. Good girl, wake up." Josie leans forward, excited.

Jean's eyes open wide for a split second, and then close again. *No. It isn't safe. Go back to sleep. Don't wake up. Brian isn't here. Gone, gone. Go back to sleep.*

Jean lies immobile again, rigid. Josie sighs. She'd been so close. She leaves the room, nodding to the guard, who sullenly follows her out to take up his position in the corridor outside Jean's room. He looks back at the bed before closing the door, as if to make sure the patient hasn't somehow been smuggled out. Once the door is closed, Jean opens her eyes again, just a crack, a tiny slit, but enough for reality to enter.

"Brian…now…I've lost you…forever," she croaks in a hoarse whisper. She looks around the room, gazes at the window, then closes her eyes again, but of her own volition this time. She tries to enter the safe place again, but can't find her way back there.

CHAPTER THIRTY-ONE

"Absit omen.
May it not be an omen."
(Latin saying)

"Will you call Judge, or shall I?" she asks, knowing the answer.

"You go on downstairs. I'll call him." He makes it sound like a favor, but she knows him well enough.

"Fine. Let me know what he says."

"Of course, darling," he says, only mouthing the "darling" part. Annie can't help laughing.

The rest of the day goes by like molasses. Duncan calls Judge, who isn't home. Nor is Josie, apparently, so he leaves a message.

It has continued to snow all day, and the wind is stinging. Wild gusts come driving in from the open sea, sweeping through the harbor, across T Wharf, and straight up Broadway. It seems a true Nor'easter is in the offing. They walk the short way home bent down, squinting.

Gussie whines pitifully as Annie gets inside the door, and she lays in a fire for him before even taking her coat off.

"You poor old thing," she says. Gussie sniffs, takes a few awkward turns inside his basket, and goes back to sleep.

"Whose turn is it to cook?" Annie says, frowning. They have been eating away from home for a couple of nights, and who can remember, anyway, with all that's been going on?

"Oh, I know! It's your turn, Dunc. I made chowder, remember, and that's the last dinner we had at home." Duncan makes a face.

"Okay, so it's my turn. How about pizza?"

"Oh, you don't have to go to that much trouble, Dunc."

"I was more thinking of calling for a take-away, or whatever it is you call it."

"A take-out? Well, that's a first. But it would suit me fine. Does that mean that you get out of cooking a dinner altogether, or do I get to order take-out tomorrow?"

"Whatever you say, my dearest girl."

"Okay, then. I'll call and put in the order, if you want. You'd never get past the list of choices for toppings." Duncan nods gratefully, and Annie dials.

"Hi, I'd like to order one large pizza, please, with artichokes, olives, mushrooms, peppers, onions and anchovies." Duncan looks happy until she gets to the anchovies. She grins at him and hangs up.

"Gotta have anchovies, Dunc. It just isn't pizza, otherwise," she explains.

"In that case, we'll need some hearty wine. Jacob's Creek Shiraz, for instance." Which, fortunately, there is some of in the likker locker, as Duncan had made the trip "out of town" to Gloucester earlier in the day.

• • •

Early in the morning, Annie crawls out of bed. It's freezing in the bedroom. They've had another power outage. Gussie is going to be livid. She pulls one of the blankets off the bed to wrap around herself. Duncan growls, feeling the sudden chill. Annie goes downstairs, pokes at the embers, and puts a couple of logs on. Gussie ignores her completely, until she pulls the blanket off her back and covers him. He turns to her and gives her a smoldering glance under half-closed eyes.

Before she leaves, she calls up the stairs.

"Dunc, I'm meeting Sally for coffee. See you in the library. It's warmer down here. I started a fire, so get up. Don't forget to call Judge." Duncan mumbles something under the remaining, obviously inadequate cover, which Annie takes to be an acknowledgement.

Fortunately, Annie and Sally get their regular table at the coffee shop. With all the goings-on, the place is already steamed up, the windows misty from all the hot breath. It's a good thing; the noise level may let them talk in peace.

"At least it's stopped snowing. The roads are awful. Matt's at home with Tim." Sally takes a bite of Nisu.

"So what happened? I didn't want to call last night; I figured you'd call me if you knew anything." Annie sips her coffee and looks around to see who else is in the coffee shop this morning. The usual crowd, so what Sally has to say comes in a whisper.

"I would have. I really have nothing new to tell you. We went to the station and talked to the chief. Tim was taken into a separate room, and a social worker came to talk to him. After that, they talked to us for a few minutes. Said not to talk to Tim about what happened to his parents yet, as if we knew anything. Then he was allowed to go back home with us."

"How is he today?"

"Tim still isn't talking. The social worker they assigned to him, Ms. Billings, said that she would stay in touch with us and stop by later in the day to monitor Tim's behavior. Social services had planned to place Tim in a foster home, but we offered to take him in. When she heard about my Brad and Ben—you know, that they're Tim's classmates and buddies and all, she decided that it might be a good idea. So he's allowed to stay with us, *temporarily,* until she gets a ruling. Ms. Billings warned us that he might have a sudden meltdown and said to call right away if that happened. But, so far, so good."

Sally speaks so quietly that Annie has a hard time hearing what she says.

"She did stop in to check on everything," Sally continues, "you know, wanted to make sure that we'd be a safe place, and to check on my boys, who behaved themselves pretty well. She's an older woman, and a little fussy about things. She checked my bathroom medicine cabinet, then went and even checked the fridge; I don't know what she was looking for. She didn't like the fact that you can see Tim's house from our windows, but on the whole, I guess we passed. She told me he wasn't to go to school yet. If he asks any questions, we're to say we don't know anything yet, but that we're sure everything will be all right. Which it won't."

"And you haven't heard anything about Lorraine?"

"The paper says Jack's dead and Lorraine's still in ICU in critical condition, recovering from surgery. There's some speculation about who shot who, which I refused to read. You know how the paper goes on. It's so sad, Annie. God, I only hope she makes it. Imagine poor Tim, if he loses both his parents. What would happen to him? Oh, and Annie, would you mind coming over tonight for a little while and stay with the boys? Matt has to work late to make up time, and I need to go to the grocery store. I don't want to leave the boys alone with Tim, in case he gets upset. How long are they planning to keep the poor kid in the dark, anyway? We can't turn on the TV or leave the newspaper around, and the boys have to watch their mouth all the time." Sally is still half-whispering, even with the din going on in the background, and Annie has to stop chewing so she can hear better. The coffee shop is filled to capacity, and people are still arriving.

"Sure, Sally, I'll be over later." Annie suddenly wonders if there had been anything in the paper about Bella. She decides that, since Sally hasn't brought it up, news probably hadn't gotten out yet. Maybe Chief Murphy has decided to clamp down on it. In any case, Annie would rather not talk about it.

Some people at the counter have been attempting to listen in, heads cocked, ears directed their way like small satellite dishes. Now, Joe Brackett walks in, bringing a blast of cold air and a puff of car fumes in with him. Mr. Lawson has left his pickup running again, right outside the coffee shop door, to warm up.

"Aw, fer Gahd's sake, shut the doah, Joe," someone shouts. Mr. Lawson hides behind his paper, pretending innocence.

Mrs. Sweeney, who is sitting right next to him, pushes his paper aside and gives him a hard stare, before she turns back to the crowd so she won't miss anything.

"I'd shut the doah if theah was standin' room in heah," Joe says, as people shuffle together to make room for him.

"Hey Joe, haven't seen you for a while. Where you been?" Billy Eakins is sitting in his usual seat, baseball cap on backwards. Considering the number of cinnamon donuts he disposes of every morning, his scrawny frame has to be considered something of a miracle. Sweeping school corridors must be quite the workout.

"Down Maine. Just got back last naht. What's all this hwite stuff aboat, then? Wintah, a'ready? Been fishin' with a pal of mahn outta Boothbay. Was suppos'ta go lake-fishin' with Larry Petersen, don'cha remembah, but he was a no-show. Got to the cabin, nob'dy theah. Ah know wheah he keeps the key, so ah went insahd. The ole potbelly was cold as a witch's tits, as they say...pahdon me, ladies. Didn' see no tracks of his cah, neithah. So ah called mah pal Jeff in Boothbay. Had a good ole time out theah instead. Good fishin' in the Gulf o' Maine, an' plenty of beah to boot. Nothin' to beat that."

Annie suddenly has a hard time swallowing. With a sinking feeling, she puts down her Nisu. She pulls at Joe's sleeve to get his attention.

"Joe, what kind of car does Larry drive?" she asks.

"An ole jeep."

Several heads turn.

"Black?" she looks at him, hoping he will say no.

Now all eyes are on Joe.

"Why? What's goin' on? Yeah, black. Why d'ya wanna know?"

"They just pulled a black Cherokee out of Steel, Joe. Is that what Larry drives, a Jeep Cherokee? There was a body in it. They haven't ID'd the body yet...face was too badly cut and swollen to recognize," Billy says.

"Whatcha sayin'? Larry drove hisself ovah the edge?"

"No, Joe, the man in the jeep was dead before he went over the edge. At least according to the paper."

"Good Lawd. You tellin' me Larry was muhde'd?"

"Ah, well, yeah...if that's who it is. Unless he drove himself in after he died," Billy says, causing some groans.

"Aw, come on, Billy, don't be making jokes about the dead," Sally says.

"Sorry, Sally."

Joe takes his wool cap off and scratches his head.

"Well, ah'll be gosh-dahn. The poah son-of-a...who the hell'd wanna do a nahs guy lahk Larry in?"

"I think we should call the police," Annie says, "before we start making any hasty assumptions. It might not even *be* Larry, but it sure sounds like it *could* be." *So much for Mrs. Ridley identifying Brian,* she thinks. If it turns out to be Larry Petersen, Mrs. Ridley will have to eat crow.

"I'll call." Alice, the part-time helper, is behind the counter this morning. She picks up the receiver and dials the police.

CHAPTER THIRTY-TWO

"Always suspect everybody."
(Charles Dickens, The Old Curiosity Shop)

The police now presume that the dead man is Larry Petersen. Joe was asked to come up to the station, where he told the chief that Larry had a tattoo on his left arm, an anchor and the initials USN, which to the chief had been an indication of it being *Brian Stokes'* body, since it had been told to him that Stokes had been in the Navy. Apparently, Larry had also been a Navy man. Joe then had been shown a photograph of the dead man's face, and looking quite shaken, he had nodded sadly. It may not be proof positive, but the chief is inclined to think that this identification is going to hold up, between the tattoo on the body and Joe's description of Larry's jeep. It appeared likely that Larry, without knowing, had bought a stolen vehicle. The ID number had been filed off, probably long ago. But the make and year of the Jeep is the same as that listed in Larry's name in the town registration rolls. Things appear to be falling into place.

When Joe Brackett stepped back outside the police station, the *Chronicle* van had been waiting, along with a few curious locals. Word will spread quickly now about the body being that of the popular hockey coach.

That puts a whole new spin on things, of course. Remembering the brawl up at the hockey rink recently, the chief realizes instantly that one logical suspect lies dead in the morgue, possibly right next to the victim. And the only person who might be able to shed light on this, the suspect's wife, is still in ICU, hovering between life and death. What about the boy, Tim? Might he know something? They'll have to check with the social worker first, to see if she thinks the boy could stand being questioned. With Judge Bradley already looking over his shoulder, Chief Murphy isn't going to do anything that would discredit the department, such as badgering a child who may have lost both his parents in an unspeakable tragedy. He'll have to tread carefully. In fact, maybe he should take the initiative and call Bradley first, kind of as a precaution.

And what about the other case, now? Does this turn of events mean that Mrs. Stokes is off the hook? Even though her husband is still missing? *Confound it.* He'll have to leave the guard on duty while he considers this.

And what about Bella? No, he'd better clamp the lid down on that for a while. Especially since she had turned out not to be dead...although she might just as well be, considering the terrible shape she is in. And even if she were to recover, you can't ever make sense of anything she says. The chief has accepted, however, that Bella may be both a witness and a victim of violence.

Well, one thing at a time. He'll start with Judge Bradley. The chief dials, but the line is busy.

Duncan has finally reached Judge and is filling him in on the news: Annie finding Bella's body; and her stunning discovery of Stokes' wife's obituary. Judge is just as surprised and shocked as Duncan had been about the obituary. Annie, of course, had been less surprised, having speculated early on that Brian was leading a double life. In her mind, the obituary only seemed to confirm her guess.

As soon as he finishes talking to Duncan, Judge puts in a call to the chief. Chief Murphy listens silently. His eyes get that faraway look again, that tired *I-don't-believe-what-I'm-hearing-what-else-can-go-wrong* look while he tries to acclimatize his brain to this new turn, coming just when he thought that everything was beginning to fall into place. He briefly informs Judge of the probable identification of Larry Petersen's body, and they both fall momentarily silent. He considers telling Judge that Bella is alive, but decides to hold off while he ponders recent developments. When Chief Murphy hangs up, he puts his elbows on the desk and braids his fingers together to rest his chin on. He closes his eyes and meditates on his options.

CHAPTER THIRTY-THREE

"You will wake, and remember, and understand."
(Robert Browning, "Evelyn Hope")

Annie gets to the library a few minutes early. While she waits for news—from Duncan, Judge, the police, Sally, anybody—she prints out the answer to last week's stumper, which she posts by the circulation desk.

• • •

LAST WEEK'S STUMPER

ANSWER: All these titles are quotations from Shakespeare:

"Brave new world" (Tempest) *How beauteous mankind is! O brave new world, that has such people in it!*

"Remembrance of things past" (Richard II) *Writ in remembrance more than things long past.*

"The sound and the fury" (Macbeth) *It is a tale told by an idiot, full of sound and fury.*

"The dogs of war" (Julius Caesar) *Cry havoc and let slip the dogs of war.*

"Something wicked this way comes" (Macbeth) *By the pricking of my thumbs, something wicked this way comes.*

"Cakes and ale" (Twelfth night) *Dost thou think, because thou art virtuous, there shall be no more cakes and ale?*

"Band of brothers" (Henry V) *We few, we happy few, we band of brothers;*

For he today that sheds his blood with me
Shall be my brother.

We had several correct answers this time. Congratulations to Wally (as usual), Karen, and Eric!

P.S.: I'll try to offer a more challenging stumper for next week! Annie.

• • •

Of course, many of the correct answers have come from people who know Annie's predilection for Shakespeare. Still, now and then she likes to get Willie into the mix. She'll have to pick something trickier for the next stumper. *I'll work on it tonight, when I get home. That is, if this day ever ends,* she thinks. Task done, she pins the stumper answer up by the main desk.

As soon as Annie sits back down, Marie transfers a phone call. It's Josie Mandel.

"Hi, Annie, I'm planning to drive over to the hospital to visit Jean. Want to come?"

Annie is shocked at Jean's appearance, not having seen her since she was carried out of the library on a gurney. Her colleague is so pale, she looks more dead than alive. Josie, on the other hand, seems encouraged by her look.

"See? I think she's coming out of it," she says.

Annie is not convinced. They sit down on either side of the bed. Josie reaches out for Jean's hand, and nods to Annie to take the other.

"Hello, Jean, it's Josie again. I have Annie with me this time. See? I went and picked her up at the library. Why don't you open your eyes and have a look?" Josie keeps talking, stroking Jean's hand, and saying anything that comes into her head just to keep a steady stream of words going.

Annie gets the idea, and takes over when Josie runs out of things to prattle about.

"Hi, Jean, I'm here, too. It's me, Annie. I brought you some flowers. Yellow roses, I know you like yellow roses, Jean. We all miss you at the library, especially Marie. She can't wait for you to come back. It's so busy behind the desk. Penny is trying her best, bless her, but we need you back, Jean." She gives Josie a quick glance. "Oh, and Jean, we've been trying to get hold of your husband," Josie tries to shush Annie now, but she carries on, "only we don't have a telephone number. Where's Brian, Jean? Can you tell us? I'm sure you want him to be here with you." Annie has to look away from that pale face, feeling insensitive and guilty at what might be a cruelty. *Well, maybe I am cruel*, she thinks, *but we need to find him, don't we, if only to clear Jean.*

"Annie, Annie, look," Josie whispers. Annie looks up at Jean's face again. Jean's eyes are open, and those lovely violet eyes are making the whole face look alive again. The eyes move slowly from Josie to Annie.

"Oh," Jean says hoarsely, and tries to clear her throat.

"Jean, I'm so glad to see you awake," Josie says, very gently, and Jean turns back to her.

"Have I been…asleep?" she whispers, and coughs a little.

"Yes, Jean, for several days. You fainted in the library, you see, and then you were brought here." Josie tries to keep it simple so Jean won't be afraid or confused.

"Days…"

"Yes, dear. How do you feel? Are you thirsty? I'll have the nurse bring you something to drink if you like." Josie looks at Annie questioningly and inclines her head toward the door.

Annie shakes her head, mouthing, "Wait, wait…"

"No…not thirsty…cold," Jean whispers. Josie takes off her shawl and drapes it across Jean's chest and shoulders. "Mmmm," Jean closes her eyes.

"Jean, where is Brian?" Josie asks.

"Oh, Brian...Brian...gone, long gone..." Her hands open and close convulsively, squeezing theirs.

Grace walks into the room, prepared to take Mrs. Stokes' vital signs. She looks at Jean, taken aback when she finds her patient looking back at her.

"How long has she been awake?" Grace asks them roughly. Then she steps up to the bed, intent on her patient only. Josie moves her chair aside to allow Grace to take the patient's wrist and start performing her duties. Jean is reluctant to let go of Josie's hand, and Josie has to use her other hand to pry open Jean's fingers.

"Only a few moments. We were just saying that we should call someone in here..." Josie says.

"Fine, fine. I'll call Dr. Kim. You two had better leave now. The doctor will need to examine Mrs. Stokes. You may call later to check on her," Grace says, sounding rather short. Then she looks at Josie and gives her a not totally unkind smile before going right back to her business. The first thing Grace does is call Dr. Kim.

• • •

Judge calls around dinnertime. Duncan answers in the living room, and Annie picks up the extension in the kitchen.

"Hi, Judge, I'm here, too," she says, not wanting them to think she's listening in.

"That's fine. Lorraine's awake, although very weak. Still critical. One bullet hit the left lung and one lodged near the heart. She said Jack shot her, but can't remember much else... said she remembers Jack crumpling on top of her, his bloody face landing right next to hers, before she fell unconscious. Then, when Chief Murphy started to ask questions about Coach

Petersen, Lorraine apparently got too upset, and the doctor stopped him."

"I should think so, if she's critical. Well. Terrible. What a terrible thing. It's a good thing the boy wasn't there to witness it," Duncan says.

"And what about Jean?" Annie is disappointed in the news so far. Larry Petersen's murder still not clinched is simply making a muddle of everything.

"It'll take some time, according to Dr. Kim. Jean mustn't be rushed. She is still in a state of confusion, and Dr. Kim says no one must question her yet. It might put her right back under, he believes. Best thing is to let her come back at her own pace, let her lead the way, say what she wants. No leading questions. So if you are willing to follow that rule, you and Josie may go back to visit her again at some point. For now, no visitors will be allowed until Chief Murphy has been able to question her. As you may imagine, that will probably be days from now."

"Is she still under guard?"

"Oh, yes. The chief has ordered that the twenty-four-hour guard be continued until further notice. I think that may last until they find her husband."

"Great. Stymied on every front," Annie says, looking vexed.

"I'm sorry, Annie. Josie feels the same way you do."

"And what about Bella? Have you heard from the chief? I can't believe that her name hasn't leaked out yet," Annie says.

"Well, they still don't even know her real name yet. Talked to the chief a while ago. There may be something about it in tomorrow's paper, but no details. You know, no name, unknown causes, or something like that, I suppose. The chief wouldn't say much." Judge says.

Annie hangs up and lets Duncan and Judge continue the conversation without her. What Judge says is true. If Jean knows about the bigamy, seeing Brian would be sure to set her back, maybe even throw her into a deeper coma, from which she might never recover. Annie feels guilty having brought Brian's name up at the visit to Jean's bedside. Now, Annie tries to imagine a plausible scenario based on the new facts. What if Jean had found out about Brian's bigamy, and that he had another family that included children, and suddenly comprehended that there were years of a separate life that he had led hidden from her? And beyond that, what if she had discovered other things that *they* did not yet know about, maybe other wives or girlfriends hiding in the wings? Had Jean then tried to commit suicide...or had Brian really tried to get rid of her? Maybe there was a whole string of dead wives. Or, Annie thought suddenly, to be perfectly fair, since Brian had not yet been found, *was it still possible that he was a murder victim, with Jean the killer?* Could Jean's coma be the result of the guilt and shock she would have felt after committing such a terrible act? It was true that these were some of the same possibilities that Annie had, albeit reluctantly, considered earlier. The difference was that now there was proof of Brian's betrayal: the other wife's obituary. But Annie still refuses to believe that Jean could be a killer.

CHAPTER THIRTY-FOUR

"There is no witness so dreadful, no accuser
so terrible as the conscience
That dwells in the heart of every man."
(Polybius, History)

"Off you go, Sal, we'll be fine here. I brought a pizza for the boys, in case they haven't had supper yet. I might have a piece, too. I didn't have time to eat." Annie hangs her jacket on a hook in the hall.

Annie joins the boys, who are watching a comedy video. The twins have received strict instructions about what kind of TV and movie fare is permissible while Tim is here, and choices are limited. Ben and Brad load up on pizza (this one does not have anchovies or olives on it, just pepperoni and cheese) while never taking their eyes off the screen. Tim accepts a piece, which he nibbles on before wrapping most of it into the napkin. He does not seem to be tuned into the movie, just sits staring into the air, sighing heavily now and then. After the boys eat, Annie asks Tim, "Want to come out to the kitchen with me, Tim? My pizza's gone cold, and I'm not sure how to use Sally's microwave." All kids know how to use microwaves, no matter what brand, just like they all know how to use every program or application ever designed for a computer. Tim gets up and follows her listlessly out to the kitchen, shuffling along in a pair of too big slippers. Annie puts her pizza in the microwave, and Tim presses the appropriate buttons. It comes out perfect, the cheese gooey but not rubbery.

"Thanks. Have a seat and keep me company? I've seen that movie too many times." she says, even though she's never seen it before.

Tim sits down at the table.

"How are you doing, Tim? Are you OK?" Annie pours him a glass of soda.

"Fine." He takes a sip of the soda. "Dad's dead, isn't he?"

Annie nods. She's a little shocked at the abrupt question, but feels she can't lie to him about this.

"I'm very sorry, Tim. This must be so hard for you. But I'm relieved to hear that your mom's condition seems to have improved a little. The doctor said she was awake." Annie doesn't want to say too much, or be overly encouraging, in case things take a turn for the worse again. But she wants to give him some hope, at least, that the mother, who probably saved his life, might make it through.

Tim puts his head on the table and covers it with his arms. When he sits up again, tears that had pooled under his eyes run down his cheeks and neck. He wipes them off angrily with the back of his hand.

"I heard them."

"Do you mean when it happened?"

Tim nods.

"Mom all of a sudden had a fit and ran off to Dad's room. That's when it started." Tim sighs, letting the air out of his lungs in a long, trembling breath.

Annie pats his arm. "You don't have to talk about it if it's too hard."

"He was drunk," Tim says matter-of-factly. "He was yelling, like he does when he's drunk. Mom was screaming, too." Tim takes a sip of soda. "I heard Dad shout that he knew all about her and Coach. *'I know you've been seeing Larry behind my back,'* he yelled. Mom screamed again and came running into the kitchen, and she just grabbed me and brought me over here. Why did she go back there? Why didn't she stay here, too?" Tim looks at Annie wonderingly.

"Tim, let's hope your mom will be OK. Maybe you'll be able to see her in a day or two. That's what you should be thinking about now, your mom getting better. I'm sure she was just doing her best to protect you. That was very brave. Now it's your turn to be brave. All right?"

Tim squirms, looking uncomfortable. Maybe she should back off a little.

Annie puts the last piece of pizza in her mouth. "Mmm, that was perfect, Tim. Thanks."

"Can I go back in with Ben and Brad now?"

"Of course. Just...don't talk to the boys about this yet, OK?"

He nods and shuffles off again, a little lighter on his feet, it seems to Annie, probably after getting all that off his chest. She hopes so, anyway, as she reaches for the phone and dials Judge's number.

Briefly and quietly, she informs Judge of what Tim had said. At the mention of Larry's name, Judge groans, knowing he'll have to call the chief again.

When Sally comes back, Annie does not tell her about the conversation with Tim. Judge had suggested that it would be better to have Tim talk to Chief Murphy first, to keep his memory as pure as possible. Annie had been on the defensive, insisting that Tim had started the conversation on his own and that she had not asked him any leading questions, and Judge had done his usual harrumphing.

• • •

At home, after parking the Mini Cooper in the driveway, she tells Duncan. Poor, neglected Duncan, who is sitting in front of the fire eating reheated pizza (with skinny, dried-up little anchovies carefully picked off and left on the side of the plate) and sipping the dregs of last night's wine bottle.

"I wonder if Tim was right," she says. "About Lorraine and Larry, I mean. That would be doubly sad. Larry was a nice guy. Doesn't that sound like a motive for murder?"

"I hope that part doesn't reach the paper, true or not," Duncan says.

"I know. That poor kid. He's going to have enough to deal with if it turns out that his dad killed Coach Petersen. After the destruction of his family life, such as it was, to have his mother branded as the cause of it all would be awful. That's what Judge said, too. He was going to talk to the chief to try to keep that part out of the news. After all, as far as the public is concerned, that brawl at the hockey rink between Jack and Coach Petersen would be a plausible enough cause for the murder all by itself. Judge promised to have a chat with Tim tonight, too, to tell him that his dad may have been wrong about his mother and the coach. Tim is a bright boy. I'm sure he'll want to protect his mom," Annie says confidently.

"He told *you.*"

"I think that was just because at that moment he needed to tell someone. He'd kept it in for as long as he could."

"I hope you're right."

Duncan picks up the wine bottle, holds it to the light, and shakes his head.

"I'd offer you zome, but 'zall gone, I zink. Wan' me t'open anubbah?" he asks, pretending to be tipsy. There hadn't been enough left in the bottle for that; besides, Duncan never drinks enough to get tipsy.

"Not for me. It would just make me maudlin right now. Hoo-boy, I just remembered."

"What?"

"I was supposed to come up with another stumper for tomorrow."

"Then I guess I'd better put on some coffee. You run along. I'm sure you'll think up something fiendish."

CHAPTER THIRTY-FIVE

"The moon is down."
(Shakespeare, Macbeth)

• • •

THIS WEEK'S STUMPER

QUESTION: Can you tell us what the following are, and where they can be found?

1. *ban-gull*
2. *chili*
3. *chocolatta north*
4. *elvegust*
5. *guxen*
6. *haboob*
7. *khamsin*
8. *mistral*
9. *purga*
10. *scharnitzer*
11. *simoom*
12. *tarantata*

Please put your answers in the
purple folder! Good hunting! Annie.

• • •

Annie crawls under the covers, exhausted. It is pitch dark out, even the moon has gone to bed. Duncan turns to her and their hands touch, but that is as amorous as they get. Sleep comes and puts a stop to the relentless squirrel cage of worries, replacing it with a restful, dream-filled mist. By morning the mist has materialized right outside their windows.

CHAPTER THIRTY-SIX

"November's sky is chill and drear,
November's leaf is red and sear."
(Sir Walter Scott, "Marmion")

"Annie, time to get up. Coffee's on."

"Can't be. I just fell asleep. See? It's still dark out."

"That's not dark, that's fog."

Annie groans. Duncan dashes back downstairs, and Annie slides out from under the covers, ever so carefully. She gives the quilt a good tug to flatten out the creases, faking the making of the bed. Pulling the curtains aside doesn't make the day any brighter; a diffuse paleness is all that enters the room. It's fog all right, so dense it looks unbreathable. And now, in late fall, there is the silence. No ropes slapping and twanging against masts, no early rising fishermen making their usual racket, throwing pails into skiffs—those big, white, five gallon plaster buckets are popular, snapped up in the swap shop at the dump the moment they appear—and starting up reluctant engines. Annie can barely see the edge of her roof below the dormer window, where a family of raccoons feasted on her Concord grapes not long ago. Winemaking will have to wait another year. Well, the early nor'easter is over, and some of the snow is already melting away. But winter is coming. She grabs her robe and makes her way to the bathroom for a quick hot shower. Maybe that will set the world aright.

Duncan knocks and, without waiting, opens the door. Annie stands there dripping, rosy and warm after the shower.

She smiles, thinking he is after *her,* but it is something else. He hands her the phone.

"For you," he says.

"Hello? Who's this?"

"My name is Paul Bentley. I'm sorry to disturb you so early in the day, but I wanted to make sure to get you before you leave for the library. Am I correct in my understanding that you work at the library with Jean Stokes? The Stokes are long-time clients of mine, and I have been trying to get in touch with her."

Annie sighs and rolls her eyes.

"Clients? Are you a salesman?" Annie quickly assumes that Bentley is one of those aggressive pitchmen that plague innocent phone owners, and nearly hangs up on him before he manages to inject a hurried answer.

"No, no, Ms. Quitnot, I've been a lawyer for the Stokes family for many years and I've been trying to reach her. I was hoping you could help me."

"I see, Mr. Bentley. Say, could I call you back in a few minutes? I just got out of the shower, and I'd like to get dressed." *And have Duncan beside me,* she thinks.

"Certainly, Ms. Quitnot, I apologize," he says and gives her his number, which she scribbles on the misty mirror. She throws her clothes on, remembers to copy the number before the mist clears on the mirror, and joins Duncan in the kitchen. He looks at her questioningly. She shrugs.

"He says he's their lawyer, but he doesn't seem to know what's happened. At least that was my impression. What am I going to tell him, Dunc? Everything?"

"First you'd better make sure he really *is* a lawyer," Dunc says, "and not some newshound."

"That's exactly what I was thinking. I'll try to look him up. Pour me some coffee, and I'll do a search." Annie sidles past him, making sure to press a thigh against his in the process, and disappears into the alcove, where she brings up the Internet—without so much as a "how-d'ye-do" to desktop-Willie, despite his wise eyes and seductive lips.

She has no trouble finding a *Paul Bentley, Atty.* in Louisville, Tennessee, and jots down the address and phone number, which is the same one he gave her. She sits back and wonders what he might really want. He said he's been the Stokes family lawyer for years—but, she wonders, *which* Stokes family? Does he actually mean Jean and Brian? Would they have kept a lawyer from Louisville all these years instead of getting someone more local? Or is he talking about someone else in Brian's family, whoever's left down there? Maybe he's Mitchell Stokes' lawyer. Maybe Mitchell got curious after Annie's phone call? Annie squirms uncomfortably in her seat. Oh, but what if he's *Brian's* personal lawyer; maybe Bentley has been sent on a fishing expedition in an effort to find out about Jean's condition, *to see if she is truly dead?* She shudders. There is simply no way to find out except to call Bentley back. She knows she should call Judge, but curiosity gets the better of her. Just as she has dialed the number, Duncan arrives with the coffee.

"Any success?" he asks, handing her a steaming mug.

"Ah," she says, wondering whether she should just hang up.

"Does that mean something like 'I just dialed his number'?"

"Oh, yes, hello, is this Mr. Bentley?" Annie makes a monkey-face at Duncan, who turns a shade darker and parks himself, arms crossed, in the doorway. "This is Annie Quitnot, returning your call. Now, just what was it you wanted to ask me about?"

"As I said, I have been trying to reach Jean. You see, I received some peculiar information recently. I cannot relate the details of this to you, but I am very anxious to discuss it with her. Have you seen her in the last few days?"

"Are you telling me that you in fact are Jean's and her husband's lawyer?" Annie asks, after which there is a momentary silence.

"I'm afraid I don't understand." Bentley says.

Annie feels exasperation coming on.

"I mean, since you couldn't reach Jean, have you tried to reach her husband?" There is a longer silence at the other end this time. "Hello, are you still there?"

"I'm afraid I'm at a loss here. I was not aware that Jean was married."

"Mr. Bentley, now *I'm* the one who is puzzled. How can you be her lawyer and not know that? I mean, how long is it since you spoke to her last?" Annie has become suspicious.

"Oh, well, it was a while ago, to be sure. But, Miss Quitnot, if you would just be kind enough to help me get in touch with her? It is rather urgent that I do so, and, unfortunately, I cannot delve into the reason for this at the moment. Jean is my client, you understand."

Jean is his client? Annie ponders that statement for a moment and makes a decision.

"Mr. Bentley, Jean is ill. She is in the local hospital in a coma. I will give you the name of someone you can call for information. His name is Judge Bradley. He has been acting on her behalf, since there was no one else to turn to at the time."

"Oh, dear me. Did she have an accident?"

But Annie isn't about to fall into that trap. Let Judge feel Bentley out and decide.

"I'm sure Judge Bradley will give you all the information you need." She gives him Judge's number and hangs up. Duncan has a pensive look that Annie has learned to recognize. He is not going to criticize her directly, but she feels his disapproval nevertheless.

"Well, that's that. We'll let Judge take care of it," she says carelessly.

"What a brilliant idea."

"Coming from me, you mean?" Annie turns wide, green eyes on him.

"Hm." Duncan isn't going to comment on that. "I just wish I'd thought of it myself, *beforehand*." That's as close to a criticism as Duncan gets. He is right, of course; she should have let Judge take care of it from the start. Now she will have to wait for a call from Judge, who is probably going to be irate. *Again.* Annie sighs.

Then the phone rings. So soon? But it's only Sally.

CHAPTER THIRTY-SEVEN

"Nothing is secret, that shall not be made manifest."
(Bible, The Gospel According to St. Luke, 8:17)

"Annie, I'm on my way to visit Lorraine. I got a call with a message to come and see her. Oh, I'm so nervous; I don't know what to say to her."

"Is she still in ICU?"

"Yes, but they said it was OK, I could come, since she asked for me. Please, Annie, could you come with me?"

Sally does sound nervous, but Annie is reluctant.

"I'm sure they won't allow more than one person to visit, especially since we're not family."

"But they said it was OK, Annie." Annie can imagine Sally squeezing the receiver and pulling at the cord. She shakes her head, but gives up.

"Well, pick me up, then. Just give me a few minutes to change."

"Sure. Actually, I'm sitting in the parking space right outside your door."

"Gee, pretty confident, aren't we?" Annie rolls her eyes. She should have guessed.

"Of course."

• • •

They take the long way around the island, through Pigeon Cove, determined to avoid the daily exodus of early morning commuters. On the main drag, lines of cars are crawling out of Rockport's narrow lanes and side streets. Bleary-eyed drivers slowly inch along on the main road out of town, migrant workers of a different kind. The back way, through Pigeon Cove, Lanesville and Riverview, is probably twice as long, but Annie and Sally will get to the hospital sooner.

"I can go and visit Jean while you you're in with Lorraine," Annie suggests.

"Oh, don't leave me alone with her, Annie, please."

"Well, we'll see what the nurse says."

The nurse nods, saying they may both go in.

"She's been asking for you, Mrs. Babson," the nurse says. "Just don't let her get upset. She's very weak. A few minutes only," she cautions.

Lorraine is hooked up to a variety of life-saving equipment. Amazingly, she seems to be breathing on her own. An oxygen tank stands by the bed, small hoses are piped in through her nose. The bullet must have just grazed the lung, Annie thinks. Lorraine casts her sad eyes at Sally, and her face crumples. Despite being pudgy, Lorraine looks rather frail today. The sick pallor in her face is telling. She must be in critical condition.

"How's Tim?" Lorraine's voice is barely above a whisper.

"He's fine, Lorraine, just fine. He's with Matt right now having breakfast."

Lorraine sighs deeply and lets out a trembling breath. She tries to move herself into a more comfortable position. The move causes her pain, and she cries out. Sally reaches for her hand.

"Are you OK?" But Lorraine moans pitifully. Sally gets up, looking worried. "I'll go get the nurse."

"Why don't you let *me* go?" Annie offers.

"No, no, I'll go." Sally looks at her pleadingly.

Annie realizes that Sally is desperate to get away and takes her place in the chair next to the bed. Lorraine has stopped moaning, but her eyes are closed and the jaws clenched. She is still in pain. Her breathing has turned shallow and raspy, and now even Annie begins to worry. She puts her hand on Lorraine's and gives it a little squeeze.

"Is the pain bad?" she asks.

Lorraine opens her eyes and gives Annie a baleful look. Then she looks away and tries feebly to clear her throat. "Annie, oh, Annie. Take care of my Tim...promise, Annie..." Lorraine's voice is barely audible.

"Lorraine, you are going to be fine," Annie says firmly, trying to sound reassuring. Lorraine takes hold of Annie's hand.

"No, I'm not. And Annie..." she coughs a little, "I shot him...I shot the son-of-a-bitch...after he shot me." Her voice has become even weaker. "I saw what...he had done to Larry..." Now Lorraine's voice dies out altogether, and her grip on Annie's hand slackens.

"Lorraine," Annie says, and pulls her hand back. She suddenly remembers the woman in the hooded parka up at Steel, when they pulled the jeep out. It must have been Lorraine. Lorraine had known, or at least suspected, that it was Larry they would find in that car even then, and seeing his dead body had made her scream. Annie hurries out of the room. She meets Sally and the nurse in the corridor.

"I think she's unconscious," Annie says, and the nurse nods.

"You'd better leave now," she says briefly, and points them toward the exit.

Sally sits down at the wheel and cries so hard that Annie offers to do the driving. Sally sobs all the way back while Annie tries to process what Lorraine told her. They go toward Sally's house, and Annie tells her to dry her tears and try to calm down before they go inside.

"If Tim sees you like that he'll think Lorraine died."

"Oh, but Annie, what if she does die?"

"She's not dead yet, Sal. She might make it yet." But Annie isn't so sure herself. *I may just have heard a deathbed confession,* she thinks. She pulls into the Babson's driveway, and Matt appears on the front step.

"Well?"

"Looks serious," Annie says, "but she's still alive. Do you mind if I call Duncan? I'll have him come and pick me up."

CHAPTER THIRTY-EIGHT

"Forbear to judge, for we are sinners all."
(Shakespeare, King Henry IV)

Duncan drives them home in silence. Annie dresses for work, and they walk over to the library. The streets have been plowed and are drying, and there's a briskness in the air. Annie sits down and busies herself with the answer to the last stumper while her internal batteries get recharged. She has plenty of real work to catch up on, but her powers of concentration are depleted at the moment. Now, what was that stumper about again? Oh, yes, ban-gull and chili…

• • •

LAST WEEK'S STUMPER

ANSWER: The names on the list refer to SMALL SCALE OR LOCAL WINDS, description and location as follows:

1. *ban-gull: summer sea breeze, in Scotland*
2. *chili: warm dry wind, sirocco, in Tunisia*
3. *chocolatta north: northwest gale, in the West Indies*
4. *elvegust: cold descending squall, in the Norwegian fjords*
5. *guxen: cold wind, in the Swiss Alps*
6. *haboob: sandstorm or duststorm, in the Sudan*
7. *khamsin: southerly desert wind, in Egypt*
8. *mistral: northwest, fall and jet effect wind, in France*
9. *purga: similar to blizzard or buran, in Siberia*
10. *scharnitzer: cold northerly wind, in Tyrol,*

11. *simoom: dry, dust-laden desert wind, in the Middle East*
12. *tarantata: northwest wind, in the Mediterranean Sea region*

Source: Our Reference 2 Vol. Set "ENCYCLOPEDIA OF CLIMATE AND WEATHER"
Okay folks, we had two correct answers—both from librarians!

• • •

When the answer is posted, she sits down to think. She won't tell anyone about Lorraine's confession, not even Duncan. Not yet. Should she tell Judge? If she did, wouldn't he be obliged to act on it? Isn't *she* obliged to? Morally, at least? But if Lorraine died, what difference would it make in the end? Except to Tim. If what Lorraine had told her were to come out, *both* his parents would be murderers. Of course, for Lorraine it would most likely be a case of self-defense, but Tim would always remember that after his father had killed his mother, his mother had killed his father. Tim might still come to miss his father, despite the faults that Jack had in abundance. The abuse and alcoholism that Lorraine had tried so hard to protect the boy from, for instance. Foolish woman, not getting help in time. Annie decides to hold off, and not even tell Judge. She'll be surprised if Lorraine survives the day.

After a while Duncan calls her up to his office.

"OK, Annie, what's going on? You're awfully quiet."

"Nothing, Duncan. Lorraine looked terrible. And I had meant to stop in to see Jean while I was at the hospital, but Sally was so upset that I forgot. Lorraine lost consciousness, which is why we had to leave in such a hurry. Did Judge call?"

"He just did. He's checking into a couple of things, but he couldn't tell us anything yet. They're coming over to our house tonight. So, on your lunch hour, could you procure some edibles to serve our guests?"

"What? Is this what I ran up here for? To get out of breath, and then sent to do chores on my scant lunch hour, and after that to be prepared to serve dinner to two guests who don't think anything of spending a whole afternoon chopping and braising and whipping and stirring and all that? And don't forget, apart from cooking the dinner I'll have to dust and vacuum and pick up dirty dishes and books and newspapers all over the house, not to mention walk the dog. And after all that, I'll have to be a gracious hostess?"

"Come on, Annie, I know you can do it. You're famous for your half-hour dinners, you know. And besides, you'll get to drive the Cooper!"

"Yay. And I thought you had some important information for me."

"But I do. Just one bit, that's all I've got. Brian's alive. That's all Judge would tell me. Apparently there's a lot more, but we'll have to wait for the rest."

CHAPTER THIRTY-NINE

"Let me sit in my house by the side of the road"
(Sam Walter Foss, "The House by the Side of the Road")

Jean dreams, wakes, wonders if anyone is in the room with her. She squints a little, just enough to check, but she's alone. She still keeps her eyes closed, just in case someone should drop in. Jean doesn't want to be surprised. How much do they know, she wonders. What had she told them in her half-conscious state? Uncomfortable memories come back to haunt her as she lies there, relentless, obsessive memories. She tries to avoid them and finally falls into an uneasy slumber. She dreams again.

Mr. Groveland, the realtor, looks at her a—little doubtfully, she thinks. She straightens in her chair.

"Well, you see, my husband is in the Navy, so I have to do this myself, buy a house, I mean. I do have references with me." She holds up a couple of envelopes.

"Oh, yes, madam, of course. Now, you see, we usually deal with both husband and wife in these situations...such a big purchase, most often the largest in a couple's life," he says. Except when you deal with the husband alone, she wants to say, but doesn't. She has expected this, of course, but won't let it deter her. She wants this very house, and means to get it.

"My husband is stationed abroad," she says, trying to put some authority into her voice, "and the house will be in my name for the time being. You don't have to worry; you'll get your money." She is surprised at how self-assured she sounds, almost forward. Not her usual shy, timid self.

"Yes, of course. Oh dear, Mrs. Stokes, please don't get me wrong. It's just a little unusual around here, that's all. We mostly know all our customers, you see. They are usually people who have grown up in town and finally become ready to buy their own home...that kind of thing. Out-of-towners most often buy the summer cottages, you see, and then some of them tear them down and build a big house there instead. You don't see many little old cottages anymore. Now, take this house here that you're interested in, for instance. There used to be an old cabin there, and somebody bought it and tore it down and built this place instead. Nothing but little old cabins up there in the woods in the old days. Part of Dogtown, then...well, it really is even now. 'Livin' in the woods,' you know, that's what summer people wanted."

She listens to the realtor's ramblings, relieved for a while that he has stopped prattling about finances. What is he so worried about, as long as she can come up with the money? It's not as if she could abscond with the house. Mr. Groveland eyes her, a little shrewdly, she thinks. He must have thought of some other clever objection to her as a possible homebuyer.

"You must understand, Mrs. Stokes, that I have other customers looking at the property. In fact, I'm waiting to hear from another couple later today," he says.

Aha, she thinks, I knew it.

"Well, Mr. Groveland. I definitely do want the house. If no one else has made a definite offer yet, why can't I just sign a purchase agreement right now and give you a check?"

Mr. Groveland seems taken aback, almost unwilling still to accept her offer. She stands her ground, stubbornly.

"What's the usual? A percentage of the asking price?" she asks. She won't even lower herself to make an offer for less, in case that might lead to another excuse.

It takes Mr. Groveland only a moment to collect himself and name an amount. "A check would be quite satisfactory, Mrs. Stokes. Please forgive any hesitation on my part just now. As I said, it is an unusual situation around here. A bank check would be required, of course." She nods. "I will get the paperwork going and shall expect you later today." She nods again, smiling just a little, before she stands and reaches out for a handshake. Mr. Groveland has a large, moist hand, with a soft grip. Papa always disliked a soft grip, she remembers. She makes her own as firm as she can, her thin fingers squeezing Mr. Groveland's fat sausage ones.

Grace comes in to check on her patient, who appears to be sleeping comfortably. Dr. Kim has informed her that he is planning to start Mrs. Stokes on a liquid diet later today, to see if she can handle it. The guard nods at Grace as she leaves, and she nods back. It's just an automatic response; she was raised to be polite. As she continues down the corridor, she frets about the unnecessary expense of leaving the guard there twenty-four hours a day to watch that poor, inert woman. What a soft job, getting paid, day after day, just for sitting in a chair. An upholstered one, at that. He's probably getting paid twice what she is. And *she* has to run off to change bedpans.

CHAPTER FORTY

"The guests are met, the feast is set:
May'st hear the merry din."
(Samuel Taylor Coleridge, "The Ancient Mariner")

"Boy, that smell is enough to make the mouth water. Do I detect the faint aroma of fish? Duncan let you out early to cook?" Judge says, walking in the door carrying a bottle of wine. Wrong color, but they'll stash it in the likker locker for next time. Annie's platter of cheese—Gorgonzola, Roquefort and Danish blue—adds to the general *odeur* in the kitchen. Pleasantly, if you like that sort of thing. Josie hangs her coat on a hook by the door and comes in to help.

"Hm. Goat, sheep, or cow, eh?" Judge says, sniffing the cheeses. "Well, here goes." He puts a goodly slab of Gorgonzola on a cracker, which immediately breaks into little pieces. "You wouldn't have a solid piece of bread, by any chance, m'dear?"

"In the freezer. I think there's a pretty solid old baguette in there that I can thaw for you."

"Hmm. Never mind. I'll just pop a piece of cheese in my mouth and then swallow it down with a cracker, I guess."

"Just as well, because the microwave is busy at the moment with these cute little spuds. I'll just go out and check on the coals, they should be about ready to go."

Josie has a gentler touch than Judge, and manages to transfer some Roquefort onto a cracker without mishap. Duncan arrives with the wine, taken out of the chiller in the store. While he pours, Annie takes the slab of beautiful, red sockeye salmon from the counter where it has been resting, perfuming the atmosphere, and goes outside and plunks the oiled fish on the grill. It won't take long, the coals are white hot, just as they should be. She puts the finishing touches on the salad, and leaves it waiting patiently with a wet paper towel over it to keep it crisp. Then she takes a sip of the wine, which is a bit on the dry side for her taste, but will be good with the fish. *Oh, the fish.* Not to worry, the salmon is perfectly grilled, and she manages to maneuver it onto the platter without having it fall apart. She snags some dill on the way up the kitchen steps—she's been successfully nursing the herb along under some twigs and burlap, but this will be the last of it—and pats it down on top of the fish. Right away, the feathery green herb wilts slightly and perfectly from the heat. To finish the garnish, she grabs the thin lemon slices and lays them down like transparent fish-scales on top of the bed of dill.

"Have a seat."

Annie lets them eat in peace, but as soon as the dinner plates are whisked away she looks at Judge.

"Well?"she says.

"Well, I talked to Paul Bentley. He's Jean's lawyer all right. Genuine article. Was her parents' lawyer when they were alive, too. Hasn't been in touch with Jean for quite a while, he said. Apparently, there hadn't seemed to be a need. Anyway, the news is that he'll be up to visit her on Friday. I told him that she's far from fully recovered, and not to expect a lucid conversation, but he's coming anyway. I'm meeting him at the hospital in the afternoon, so we'll have to go from there."

"But nothing new about Brian? I thought you said there was a lot more," Annie says, giving Duncan an accusing glance. He shrugs. Judge harrumphs, apparently not eager to divulge any more information than he already has. He relents a little, and makes one small addition.

"Well…apparently, Bentley tried to call Brian, but one of the children answered. Naturally, he wasn't about to question the child, but that's how I know that Brian's alive; the child told him that his father was at work. Bentley said he would try calling Stokes again later, but he seemed a bit close-lipped about it. I suppose he wants to see Jean before saying anymore."

CHAPTER FORTY-ONE

"What other dungeon is so dark as one's own heart!
What other jailer so inexorable as one's self!"
(Nathaniel Hawthorne, The House of Seven Gables)

Lorraine has been scheduled for another emergency surgery. The bullet that had initially lodged near the heart suddenly appears to be on the move, and the medical team has decided on what is probably a last ditch effort to save her life. Sally calls Annie to tell her about it.

"Tim has locked himself in the boys' bedroom and won't come out. Chief Murphy called the social worker in the morning, insisting that he needed to talk to Tim, and Ms. Billings agreed. She said Tim was probably ready to be told and said she'd meet him at our house. I let them in and took them to the boys' room, and then I waited outside the door to make sure Tim would be okay. Ms. Billings sat down with Tim and told him he had nothing to worry about. Then she looked out through the door at me and said she'd leave the door open, but she'd appreciate it if I would let them talk to Tim privately. So, I went out into the kitchen, and I didn't hear much of what they said, except I heard Chief Murphy begin talking to Tim about what happened to his parents that night. Ms. Billings has such a light voice, you know, I couldn't hear her at all. They stayed a while. I don't know what else they talked about or if the chief asked Tim any questions. Anyway, they left, and as soon as the front door closed, Tim slammed his door, too, and locked it." Annie can tell by her tone of voice that Sally is frantic.

"I'll stop over after work, I promise. I'm sure he'll calm down, Sal. But how come you have a lock on the boys' door?"

"Oh, I know, I know...I knew right when we moved in to the house that we should take that lock off, but you know how it is—too many other things to do first. And our boys never even noticed it was there. Who in the world would put a lock on a bedroom door? Anyway, I tried to make Tim open the door, but he started throwing things around in there, so I said, 'Okay, okay, it's okay, Tim. Take your time.' Oh, I don't know what to do. Should I call Ms. Billings, you think? This is probably that meltdown she was warning me about. Poor kid. I'm sure he's convinced that Lorraine isn't going to make it," Sally says.

"He's probably right, too."

"And then he'll be sent into foster care. Doesn't seem fair, does it?"

Annie has thought about this.

"Would you consider taking him, Sally?" There is a short silence. Then Sally clears her throat, to let Annie know she is still there.

"Don't think I haven't thought about it, but we couldn't, Annie. Remember how it used to be, Matt and me and the boys, a regular three-ring circus? We've just got that all ironed out. It wouldn't be fair to the boys to risk it again. Tim's going to need a stable situation and a lot of care, and I'm not sure I'm the right person."

Annie feels a heroic impulse to offer to take Tim herself, assuming Duncan would go along, but she is beginning to feel rather ghoulish about the whole thing. Lorraine is still alive, after all. Annie thinks about that. If Lorraine dies, who shot Jack will be a moot point. If she survives, she will have to live with that knowledge for the rest of her life. So will Annie, for that matter. What would that do for their relationship in the future? She shakes her head. Not something she is going to think about right now.

"Sal, got to go. I see a reference question walking this way. See you after work."

"You're a doll, Annie."

The "reference question" in question turns out to be interesting. Vera, aide to the town clerk at town hall, reports that she has taken an out-of-state phone call recently regarding Jean Stokes. Annie sighs.

"Was it by any chance a call from a lawyer?"

"No, I don't think so. At least the person didn't identify himself as one."

"Maybe a reporter then?"

"Don't know, Annie. Could be, I suppose. But he asked mostly general questions, stuff you could find in the nosy pages. Wanted to know her address, marital status, job, anything he could legally find out. He sounded pretty curious about the fact that Mrs. Stokes was listed as married when the census didn't show a *Mr.* Stokes."

"Well, they're not the only people with that arrangement. Several other people on the rolls have more than once residence and register separately. So, Vera, did he leave a name and number?"

"Nope. Said he'd be stopping by in a couple of days anyway."

"Could be a reporter trying to get a story. Or maybe her lawyer. He's supposed to come later in the week." Annie is sorry the minute it slips out.

"Why?" Vera turns her questioning blue eyes on Annie. *So, this is the reference question.* The townies are curious about what is happening, and Vera has volunteered to try and find out.

"No idea, Vera. To help Jean handle her affairs, I suppose." Annie smiles her usual pleasant smile that lets a patron know she has nothing more to say on the subject, remembering somewhat uneasily the smile she'd been given by the desk nurse at the hospital. Vera looks a little irritated, but smiles back.

"Thanks, Annie. As usual, you're a fount of information."

You can cut the sarcasm with a knife, but Annie doesn't care. She'll do her best to provide people with the information they seek, but she'll never be part of the gossip circuit. She can't help wondering, though, about the phone call they'd received at town hall. If it *had* been Mr. Bentley, he would certainly have identified himself. No reason not to, since he really is her lawyer. And besides, Judge already gave Bentley all the information he asked for, of that she was sure.

Annie has a momentary urge to call Judge and tell him about Lorraine's confession, but it passes.

CHAPTER FORTY-TWO

"Where is the wisdom we have lost in knowledge?
Where is the knowledge we have lost in information?"
(T. S. Eliot, "The Rock")

Judge finally calls Duncan with word that Lorraine made it through the operation. The next twenty-four hours will be critical, he adds.

Duncan drops her off at the Babson's. When Sally opens the door, Annie can tell that things have not improved here. Ben and Brad are sitting at the kitchen table, leaning over homework. A morgue-like silence hangs over the place until a kettle whistles shrilly on the stove.

Annie pours the tea, but they forgo the usual unison quote: *'Let it be noted that Annie poured.'* An ominous silence emanates from the boys' room, and Annie points a thumb in that direction, eyebrows raised in question.

"Haven't heard a sound since I called you. I'm really worried, Annie. I almost called the chief just before you came. I did call Ms. Billings earlier, but she was out of the office. I didn't leave a message on her machine."

"Do you mind if I go and knock on the door? Just to see if I can get a reaction out of him, I mean."

"Feel free. I've tried several times. Not a peep. Can't even hear him moving around in there. I'm hoping maybe he's just asleep. I mean, he must be exhausted, with all that's going on."

Annie puts her cup down and walks over and knocks on the door.

"Tim? It's me, Annie. I brought some pizza. Want me to heat a slice for you? You must be hungry. I'm pretty sure I remember how to use their microwave now, thanks to you." She realizes she is babbling and shuts up. Suddenly there is a crash against the door; something heavy has been thrown at it. Annie takes a step back.

"Tim, are you okay?"

"Go away. I just want everybody to stay away from me." There is a tense, high-pitched edge to his voice, whether of panic, pain, or sorrow, she doesn't know.

"What's got you so upset, Tim? What did they tell you?" Annie stands close to the door, speaking softly. She isn't going to give up without a fight.

"Shut up!" His voice is totally uncontrolled now and breaks, the way a boy's voice does at that age.

"If I promise not to ask any questions or talk about it, will you let me get you some dinner? I'll just pass it to you, and then I'll leave you alone."

"No."

"We heard from the hospital, Tim. Your mom made it through the operation and is resting right now. Did you know?" Running footsteps on the other side and the sound of Tim unlocking the door make Annie scuttle backwards. The boy is a wild vision in the doorway, hair matted, clothes sweaty and disheveled.

"I don't care! I don't care about *her,* don't you understand? She killed my Dad!" he shrieks.

Annie takes a step forward, hoping to take hold of him and help calm him down, but he turns around and runs back into the room. Annie hurries after him, wanting to stop him from whatever he is planning to do. It looks like a bomb has struck in there. When she gets near him, he turns on her with a fury. She should have remembered that he is a hockey player, not just the weak, sad little boy he had appeared to be the last few days. He is strong, and his arms are flailing like windmills. She is taller and thinks she can throw her arms around him and hold him fast, but she is wrong. He has something in his hand and swings his arm at her, hitting her on the jaw with whatever it is, something hard and heavy, and she crumples on the floor. The old hockey trophy lands next to her.

Ben and Brad, hearing all the noise, come running and throw themselves on Tim, pinning him to the floor. Annie crawls away, heading for the doorway.

"Call the poleesh," she croaks. Blood is filling her mouth, and she spits on the floor, aghast when she sees the red stain on Sally's pale gold carpet. "Oh, shorry 'bout the mesh, Shal..." she says, trying to swallow the blood.

Sally runs for the phone, wailing. Annie manages to get hold of herself and hobbles back into the boys' room, where the bedlam continues unabated. Between the three of them, they manage to wrap Tim in a sheet, and then Annie and Brad keep him pinned to the floor by sitting on him, while Ben runs for something to tie him up with.

If this is a meltdown, Annie thinks, *I'd hate to see a full-fledged burst of rage.* It seems to take forever, but Ben returns with a ball of Sally's green garden string, which they laboriously wind around the still screaming Tim, making him look not unlike King Tut. They hoist him onto the bed and stand back cautiously, ready to fall on him again if he tries to break loose. Meanwhile, Tim has continued screaming and hollering. Maybe they should have gagged him, too.

"She killed my dad! Don't you see? She killed him, and then she tried to hurt herself to make it look like he did it. My dad was the one who cared about me. She didn't! She just wanted me to get good grades and go to college! Ugh! College, who cares! Dad was real proud that I was a good hockey player, but

Coach wouldn't even let him come to watch! Coach wrecked everything! And then she killed Dad!" he repeats, turning himself into a spring and bouncing himself up and down on the bed.

"But, Tim, that just isn't true. The police say your dad tried to kill *her,* and then he killed himself…" Annie tries, between his yowls and groans. Despite Lorraine's confession, she is sticking to the official storyline, just trying to slow Tim down a bit. Sirens can be heard outside now, and Tim's eyes get steely. He screams, trying in vain to break his bonds. They can hear the slam of the front door, and the sound of the chief's voice. Tim rolls himself off the bed and tries again to break out of his cocoon.

"Dad would never kill himself, never! *She* did it. I know it! And *he* didn't kill Coach! *I did!*" Tim howls.

Annie hears running footsteps in the kitchen, and Chief Murphy and Sergeant Elwell appear in the doorway.

"Okay, everybody, please leave the room. Hurry. We'll handle him." The chief had heard Tim's last outbreak and looks grimmer than ever.

Annie herds Ben and Brad out into the kitchen. Officer Elwell shuts the door behind them.

When the door finally opens, a handcuffed Tim is shuffling along between the chief and Elwell. He seems to have neither the energy nor the will left to fight. He looks down at the floor as he is led away, without making eye contact, even with the boys. Silence settles over the kitchen until the cruiser pulls away.

"Mom, do you believe him? Do you believe Tim really could have killed the coach?" Ben asks. They are all stunned by this possibility.

"I don't know, Ben, really I don't." Sally sighs. "I know that Tim loved his dad above everything. And I know that Tim and his mom have never gotten along very well. Like he said, she's always tried to make him into something he's not, you know? The boy isn't interested in academics, anybody could tell that. And his dad *was* proud that Tim was good at sports. And I have to admit that his mom just sneered at that, as if that wasn't good enough for a son of hers." Sally shakes her head before she continues her thought, talking mostly to herself. "Which is why it seems so unlikely that she and Larry would have ...been seeing each other. A hockey coach, when she was married to a successful businessman...I don't know. But, I suppose maybe it's possible that Tim could have...what he said. Larry barred Jack from the rink for the rest of the year, after all, and that was probably enough provocation for Tim. Dear God, what a tragedy." Sally has no tears left, and the boys sit quiet, looking stricken. Suddenly Sally jumps out of her chair.

"Annie! Holy mackerel, look at you! What happened to your face? Did he do that?"

"No, Shal, I did that to myshelf. What do you shink?" Annie carefully runs her fingers over her chin and lips and nose. "Good Lord, I'm a mesh, aren't I. Let me go and wash my faish."

"Never mind washing your face, I'm taking you over to Emergency right this minute. You might have a broken jaw, loose teeth, or worse!"

Annie sighs. The side of her face aches, one of her teeth does feel a little wobbly. *Oh no, does this mean yet another visit to Dr. Treadwell?* And her lips must look like those big, red wax ones they used to get at Halloween. Just then Matt walks in the door. After recovering from shock on hearing about the evening's events, he says he'll stay home with the boys and help them try to sort out their room while Sally drives Annie to the hospital.

"No, no, Shally's in no shtate to drive, Matt. We have to call Duncan firsht, anyway. He'd get pretty mad if I didn't tell him what happened, and I'm sure he'll come and take me over there. After telling me what a twit I am, trying to take Tim on, that ish." She sighs

"I guess things could have gone worse," Matt says. Quite an understatement, coming from Matt.

CHAPTER FORTY-THREE

"So I awoke, and behold it was a dream."
(John Bunyan, Pilgrim's Progress)

Jean dreams.

"I'm gonna sit right down and write myself a letter,
And make-believe it came from you..."

Sinatra with the golden voice croons the tune, melting her heart as only Frankie can. She turns the volume up and waltzes around the kitchen, humming along with him. When the song ends, she plops down in a chair, exhausted. That's when the thought hits her. Yes, why not? It will dispel her loneliness, at least for the moment. She loves her new home and has fixed it up so nicely, but it is terribly lonely here without Brian. He is still in the Navy, far away somewhere, she doesn't even know where anymore. So she sits right down and writes herself a letter—a love letter, of course—imitating his handwriting quite well, she thinks.

It's the first of many. Soon, she has a whole stack, tied around with ribbon. She includes the yellowed envelope Brian had actually sent her himself, right after he shipped out, which had been posted in Guam. She caresses his handwriting briefly with her fingertips before putting the envelope at the bottom of the pile, lending an air of authenticity to the whole collection.

Mrs. Stokes looks serene tonight. Maybe she is truly improving, Grace thinks, just before Jean starts moaning and twisting in her bed. Grace sighs and pats her arm.

"It's all right, Mrs. Stokes."

It was all a lie, wasn't it?

And that letter from Guam had started it all. That's why she had thrown the letter away and only kept the envelope.

Grace shakes her head, wishing Mrs. Stokes would wake up. Should she try to wake her out of those bad dreams? What on earth could it be that has her patient so bothered? Grace figures that her patient is no longer wanted for murder, since the body they found in the quarry didn't turn out to be her husband. She lifts Jean's thin arms and smoothes out the sheet beneath them. Then, she takes a damp, cool washcloth and mops the poor woman's face.

"Mrs. Stokes? Jean? Are you awake?" she says quietly.

Mrs. Stokes does not respond; she is back in her dream world. She seems a little calmer now. Maybe it's a nicer dream. Grace finishes her chores and leaves quietly. When she passes the nursing station, she sees a distinguished looking gentleman talking to Nurse Safford, who is pointing down the corridor while taking to him. When he moves along, Grace walks up to the desk and asks as casually as she can: "Is that man on the way to visit Mrs. Stokes?"

Nurse Safford nods, without looking up from her paperwork. *Must be the lawyer, then.* Grace had felt compelled to check, since the guard had not appeared outside Mrs. Stokes room this morning. According to Dr. Kim, Chief Murphy had called to inform them that the guard was no longer considered necessary. Still, Grace feels a little concerned, especially now that a stranger has finally turned up. However, she has other tasks to run to, and hurries along down the corridor.

In her room, Jean's mind is unsettled, as if looking for a comfortable memory to home in on.

She is cooking fish today. Not Brian's favorite fish dish, which is baked haddock with crab and breadcrumb stuffing, no, this is just a homely filet of sole. Haddock is too expensive these days, even in this little fishing village. She takes great care not to break the thin fillets when she flips them in the pan. To go along with the fish, she has made Lyonnaise potatoes and a green salad—all green: lettuce, cucumbers, green peppers, and scallions. Brian likes what he calls her "artistic touch."

She checks her watch. He is late today. Tied up in traffic, maybe. She hums a tune, covering the platter loosely with foil. Then she sits down to wait.

But Brian doesn't come.

He never did, did he?

It has all been a lie.

A big, beautiful lie.

"Jean, are you asleep?" The man pats her arm to let her know he is there. She stirs, but doesn't open her eyes.

"Jean, why didn't you tell me?" He sounds distraught, maybe even angry. She is probably listening, he thinks, and just pretending to be asleep. He gets up and walks over to the window and looks out at the view. So, this is New England in the fall. How dreary. To get here, he had driven through flurries of snow that had turned into sleet as he neared the coastline. He had shivered, going from the car to the hospital entrance. Stark, leafless trees surrounded the parking lot, brown leaves lying splattered all over the ground. Remnants of snow clung to one side of the tree trunks, and heaps of snow surrounded the parking lot. A chilly, miserable wind had nearly pulled the door out of his hand, and the wet leaves that had clung to the bottom of his shoes had transferred themselves to the polished linoleum floor in the lobby. He had looked around sheepishly, to see if anyone had noticed. Since he hadn't seen any wastebaskets around, he had left the leaves where they were.

The view from the window is cheerless, just a blank wall across from the narrow delivery alley. It has started sleeting again, and the melting slush is running down in rivulets on the windowpanes. This was the part of the country that Jean had chosen to move to. Didn't she ever miss Tennessee?

When he turns around again, he finds her eyes resting on him. As soon as she sees him look at her, her eyes close again. But he is wise to her now.

"Jean, you should have told me."

"What? What should I have told you?" Her voice is sharper than he remembers and surprisingly strong, coming from such a weak and helpless looking creature.

"That we are not cousins. That you were adopted."

She opens her eyes now, lets them remain open. The big, violet eyes that he had remembered so fondly, and with so much regret, for so many years. Eyes, whose owner, he had been told—by his own mother, no less—would never belong to him. Jean's eyes are ageless. As he looks into them now, they are just the same today as they had been that day long ago, in that restaurant down in Knoxville, when she had accepted his ring.

"Because of Mama."

"Because of *your* mama?"

Mr. Bentley, when he called, had briefly brought him up to date about Jean. The lawyer had first told him that she was very ill, lying in the hospital in a coma, although apparently beginning to come out of it. Bentley had then told him a number of other things: that both her parents had passed on; that the old house had been sold; and that Jean had used her inheritance to buy a house up here in New England. Bentley had also mentioned—as if in passing—the fact that Jean had been illegitimate, but that hadn't meant a thing to Brian at the time. It had just been a curious bit of information, which he hadn't given much thought to then, having been too concerned about Jean being ill and apparently all alone. Admittedly, he had been mystified by what his own role in the situation was supposed to be, wondering why Bentley had called him out of the blue like that. After all, he hadn't seen or heard from Jean since his Navy years.

Now, suddenly, the light dawns.

"You mean...it would have caused your mother shame if it had come out? Is that it? The fact that someone else, not your father, made her pregnant, and she didn't want it to be known? And so you gave me up. To save your Mama's reputation."

Jean nods tiredly.

"What difference does it make now, Brian?"

"But, Jean, if you had told me, at least...and Jean," he adds, hesitating a little, "is it possibly true that you've lived your whole life pretending to be married to me?" That's what Bentley had suggested to Brian, who had thought it preposterous. Then, when Brian had called the local town hall, the woman he spoke to had been firm about Mrs. Stokes marital status. "*Yes, we've had a listing for Mrs. Stokes, Mrs. Brian Stokes, for many years.*"

"No, Brian, not really. I didn't *pretend.* At least not as I saw it. You see, I *was* married to you. Forever. There was never anyone else. And until recently, nobody ever bothered me about it. It started with the census lady. She kept asking questions and then, when I went to town hall to pay my real estate tax, someone in the assessors' office also inquired about you. After that, I began to think about how I'd been living my life. I started to believe I was losing my mind. And then, that day in the library...when I fell, or fainted, or whatever it was...oh, I remember now...I had just finished checking in a book, and the title of it was *Beautiful Lies,* and it struck me all at once: *that is all my life has been. A big, beautiful lie.* I don't remember anything after that. I'm sorry you had to come all this way, Brian, and find out about this. It must be very unpleasant for you. Did Uncle Paul call you? Mr. Bentley, I mean."

"Yes, he did. When I told him I wanted to go and see you, he wasn't sure it was such a good idea. He tried pretty hard to talk me out of it, actually. Oh, Jeanie-girl, what a mess."

"Brian, I'm so very sorry that you had to come. It must be very awkward for you. I know you're married...I've managed to find out little bits about you now and then, you see. And you have children, too. Oh, you shouldn't have come. Your wife must think it awfully strange. If you told her where you were going, that is."

"I guess you haven't found out *all* the little bits about me, Jean. I'm a widower, you see. My children are spending a few days with an aunt while I'm away. If my wife had still been alive, I *would* have told her. I loved my wife, Jean. She was a lovely person. You would have liked her." He looks down at his hands.

Jean is too exhausted to cope with this thought. When Brian looks back up at her, she is asleep.

CHAPTER FORTY-FOUR

"When the head aches, all the members partake of the pains."
(Miguel de Cervantes, Don Quixote)

Duncan takes one look at Annie and doesn't get mad. Instead, he gives her a powerful embrace, closing his eyes in relief. The outcome could have been far different. On the way to the hospital, she tells him what happened.

"I should have figured it out, Dunc. Lorraine would never go for somebody like Larry, even Sally sensed that. Hockey, fishing...could you see it? Jack was a solid provider. I'm sure she figured that she could eventually work things out so that her Tim would end up in college. Jack was just drunk, taunting her, trying to get her sidetracked. It must have been just the usual thing with them."

"Annie, it'll probably all come out in due time, you know how it is. Try to relax, sit back, and think about something else. For instance, guess who called me just before you did?"

"Who? Judge? Oh, Duncan, what a nitwit I am! We have to call Judge! He has to go and help Tim...Tim doesn't have anyone now, maybe Judge can represent..."

"I'm way ahead of you, love. I took care of it as soon as I hung up after Sally's call. Now, calm down a little. Where was I...oh yes...well, you'll never guess, so I'll tell you who called. Brian Stokes. And now for the really big news. Mr. Stokes is in town. You're going to meet him."

"But, Duncan, what on earth..."

"That's all, m'love, all I have. I know nothing beyond that. You'll have to wait until tomorrow for the rest."

It's after eight, and the side emergency door is closed. They pull into the hospital parking lot and walk in through the main entrance. Usually, a varied and sometimes colorful collection of injuries and complaints line the waiting room, but Annie is in luck tonight. She'll get to see the doctor on duty as soon as she has gone through all the usual formalities: show her hospital card, fill out the forms, give the insurance information, and anything else that could cause a seriously ill person to expire on the spot. As she is taken away, Duncan assures her he'll be right there in the waiting room when she is through.

When the doctor on call walks into the examination room, his eyebrows lift.

"Oh dear, what happened here?" Annie is caught speechless. She hadn't thought of how to explain her injuries. What could she say? That she'd had a fight with a teenager who had just confessed to being a killer? But, apparently, the physician isn't really interested in the answer. He gets busy cleaning the blood off her face, palpitating her jaw gently, and checking her teeth.

"Hmm. I'm sending you over for an x-ray. Don't think there's anything broken, but we want to make sure. One of your teeth has loosened, but it may settle. I advise you to go and see your dentist, though."

Annie considers this. *Oh, Dr. Treadwell will be so excited to see me.* The doctor gives her a form to bring along to radiology, and then he touches the side of her face with his forefinger. "You will most definitely have some bruising along here. Quite a bit, as a matter of fact. Taking up boxing, are we? Next time, wear headgear."

He probably assumes this is a case of spousal abuse, Annie thinks.

"It was an accident, that's all. Honest."

"Right. To get to radiology, go through this corridor here and then take a left."

"Thanks, Doc, I've been there before."

"I'm sure you have."

Annie gives up, and Duncan tags along with her over to the radiology lab. When she is through, the technician tells her she will have to wait for the results until she speaks to the doctor, which is the usual routine. Duncan drives them home.

"Hungry? Did you have something to eat over there?"

"Nope. Brought a pizza, but I never got to eat any of it."

"I'll fix you a sandwich if you like," Duncan offers.

"If you premasticate it for me, maybe," she says, testing her jaws.

"Ugh. How about a cup of chicken soup, then?"

"That cures everything, doesn't it? Why have I never liked chicken soup? I think it's those mushy vegetables and the overcooked pasta."

"Just the thing, then, isn't it? No need to chew."

"I guess."

She manages to down a cup of canned chicken noodle soup, shuddering at the slimy texture. Like swallowing little polliwogs. Just as she is climbing into bed, slowly and carefully, since her head has begun to ache, the phone rings. Duncan answers. It's Judge, who has been keeping in touch with the chief. Annie lies back on the pillow. Her head is pounding. Duncan takes the cordless receiver along downstairs, waving to Annie to go to sleep.

CHAPTER FORTY-FIVE

"There was so much handwriting on the wall
That even the wall fell down."
(Christopher Morley, Around the Clock)

"Well." Duncan says, as he sits down on the side of the bed. "Tim confessed to killing the coach. With his hockey stick, no less. Apparently, Lorraine found a charred piece of it in the fireplace the night of the shooting. Tim said his father helped him to cover up the killing by getting rid of the body. Jack drove Larry's jeep up to the quarry, Tim said, and helped it over the edge. Jack also tried to hide the evidence by burning the hockey club, Tim went on. Guess he didn't make sure it had all burned." Before continuing, he takes Annie's hand, hearing a soft sob.

"Then, Judge said, the chief asked Tim if he had killed the witness, too, and apparently Tim seemed taken aback for a moment, before he said, 'Of course I did.' But when the chief asked him what he had done with the body, Tim said that he had 'dumped him in the quarry.' Apparently, without knowing anything about it, Tim quickly assumed that his dad must have killed an eyewitness up there and then guessed that Jack would have gotten rid of him right on the spot." Duncan pauses while Annie, frowning, tries to absorb all this.

"Well, by then, the chief was beginning to wonder, I guess, about Tim's whole confession. And when pressed, and after being told what really happened to the witness, Tim broke down and blurted out the real truth. The long and the short of it is: Tim didn't kill the coach, Jack did. Tim came along when Jack drove over to the coach's house, ostensibly to apologize. Jack left Tim sitting in the car while he went and knocked on the door, determined to make Larry change his mind about barring him from the games, Tim said. Unfortunately, Jack must have been in his usual state, and when Larry wouldn't back down, well, Jack came running and swearing out of the house, grabbed Tim's hockey stick out of the trunk, and went back inside. Tim heard shouts, and then Jack came out and threw the broken hockey stick back into the trunk before tearing off. He'd brought it along for the purpose, I imagine. Then, Jack dropped Tim off at home and took off again, telling him he had an errand to do. Obviously, he went back to Larry's house and loaded the body into the Jeep...and the rest we can imagine."

Annie closes her eyes, and Duncan squeezes her hand. He waits until she opens her eyes again, nodding for him to continue.

"Well, Chief Murphy's theory after that is that poor Bella watched Jack push the Jeep over the edge into the quarry and that Jack caught sight of her. He must have chased her all the way to the Tool Company to take care of her there. That's conjecture, of course. We may never know for sure. But Tim is completely innocent. He tried his best to defend his father's actions. 'He did it for me,' he cried."

Annie looks at him, aghast. "Oh, Dunc, how awful. The poor kid."

Duncan wraps his arm around her back. "Do you want to hear the rest? Tell me if it's too much for you," he says.

"Tell me everything, Duncan. I need to get everything out in the open, so that I can deal with it and put it behind me."

Duncan nods. "Judge said the police knew when they saw her that what happened to Bella wasn't an accident. Apparently, they found blood in several places inside the forge. So when Tim professed that he had killed the witness, too—to protect the image of the dad he idolized, I suppose—well, that's when the chief got suspicious. And when Tim continued by saying that he'd 'dumped him in the quarry,' the chief knew, of course."

"Poor Tim. Can you imagine the stress that kid must have been under, knowing that his dad had killed the coach? And poor, stupid Jack, to be so suspicious of Lorraine. And poor Larry. And poor Bella. And poor Lorraine. Poor, poor Lorraine. Can you imagine what her life is going to be like now? What will..."

Duncan interrupts her.

"Here, I made you a cup of tea. Do you think you can drink it or is it too hot?" Duncan puts a mug down beside her.

"It's lovely. Thanks, my very dear man. Oh, and poor Jean. I wish I knew how she's doing."

"Of course. We'll know more tomorrow, Judge promised to keep us informed."

"Dunc, I'm so incredibly sorry I got us involved in this mess."

"Well, darling, we don't know whether it changed the outcome of anything, do we? Now, go to sleep. Tomorrow is another day."

"Annie, the chief is here, says he'd like a word...are you asleep yet?" Duncan calls up the stairs an hour later. Annie's still awake and sits up, trying to catch her bearings.

"I'll be right down, just got to slip into something..." she says, getting into a pants and a sweat shirt before hurrying downstairs. Chief Murphy and Duncan are seated in the dining room. Duncan gets up and pulls out a chair for her.

"Ms. Quitnot," the chief says, "didn't realize that you'd been injured in that tussle with the boy...hope you're feeling better than you look. You've been into some dangerous situations lately…you should be more careful, you know. In fact, I'm here because I got a call from the repair shop in Pigeon Cove a while ago. You were at the hospital, so I couldn't reach you until now. Well, it appears that the accident with your car may not have been an accident after all…they tell me that the car had been interfered with, causing your brakes to fail."

Annie sits thunderstruck for a moment. Then she remembers the cannonball ride in her Chevy down Landmark Lane, when she had been wondering if she was about to hurtle into the sea like one of the old quarry locomotives. She hadn't had any trouble with the brakes before, which crew at the repair shop had thought odd. And then she recalls the noise she thought she had heard at the Tool Company, and the shadow she had seen in the window. Afterwards, she had been sure it was her imagination. Now she sees it differently: *It must have been Jack*. Jack had come back to dispose of the body, and she had surprised him.

When she finishes telling the chief, he nods.

"That seems to fit with a report by someone who lives next to the Tool Company, who said he'd seen a boat tied up to the pilings underneath the forge, which he thought was strange. Davis probably meant to drop her into the boat through one of those holes in the floor," the chief suggests. *And deep-six her out at sea*, Annie thinks. "Then, afraid that you might have seen and recognized him, he came after you. Well, you probably saved Bella's life, you know," the chief says at last, and both Annie and Duncan look startled, until the chief tells them of Bella's possible recovery.

CHAPTER FORTY-SIX

"No creature smarts so little as a fool."
(Alexander Pope, "Epistle to Dr. Arbuthnot")

The library closes early on the day before Thanksgiving to give staff time to go turkey hunting, grind the cranberry-orange relish, and whatever other homely chores they might think of. Annie's bruises haven't quite faded yet, but at least people have stopped asking what happened to her. The word has gone full circle, and the coffee shop has been doing a brisk business lately. The latest news is out: Bella is alive and will recover...well, to her previous state, anyway. Annie takes Esa to visit her, and he brings one of his usual fairytale bouquets and a homemade card. Annie waits outside, feeling the two would be more comfortable without her. Bella will surely be visiting the library soon enough, and Annie will be glad to welcome her back. And the chief sees no need to use Bella as a witness, which is a relief.

Lorraine is still in the hospital, but is also going to live. Whether she has the *will* to live is another question. The apple of her eye is going to need a lot of loving care, and the husband who had accused her of two-timing him had never understood that despite all his faults, she would never have cheated on him. Thanksgiving is going to be a bitter holiday for Lorraine Davis, spent recovering in the rehab facility adjoining the hospital. The librarians have sent her a fruit basket with a couple of gentle books tucked in, and Marie has quietly suggested to a few caring townies that a little bouquet of flowers or a get-well card might be appreciated.

Tim is heading for some serious therapy. At the moment, that's where Annie leaves off thinking about it. They will all need time to get a perspective on things.

Brian had arranged, after his first visit to the hospital, to prolong his stay at the motel for a couple of weeks in order see Jean through the early stages of therapy. He had made a phone call to the aunt and explained as much as was necessary about the needs of an old friend, and she had been delighted to be in charge of the children a little longer.

Tomorrow they will all gather at Judge and Josie's for a potluck Thanksgiving dinner, Jean, Brian and Uncle Paul included. Josie is doing the turkey, which leaves everyone else free to experiment with the sweet potato marshmallow pie and other typical New England conundrums. Duncan has promised to take care of his and Annie's share of the duties, and is no doubt planning something unusual, as usual.

Jean already has made great strides, doubtless at least in part due to Brian's presence and encouragement. Annie feels none too clever when she remembers her own deductions regarding Brian. *A bigamist!* When Judge first informed her of the strange truth of the matter, Annie had been aghast. For a fleeting moment she had thought of Mrs. Ridley...was she becoming like her? Well, it had all seemed logical at the time.

Annie checks her watch. A couple of hours until closing. She makes a few calls to remind forgetful students to pick up the information or inter-library loans they have requested, items they will need to finish projects during the holiday. Duncan comes trotting down the stairs, but, instead of heading toward her desk, he walks out through the main entrance. When he comes back in, he is accompanied by a pale but surprisingly healthy-looking Jean, who is leaning on the arms of two staunch supporters: "Uncle Paul" and the long mythical Brian Stokes, the man whose absence had started the whole thing. When Paul Bentley, now an elderly, retired lawyer, arrived, he had been astonished to find Brian at the hospital ahead of him. Fortunately, Jean had been sufficiently improved by then to explain everything to him, although it had taken a couple of visits. Dr. Kim had been stern about keeping visits short and had not wanted to see his patient in an emotional state.

Who knows what will come of it all? *They do make a sweet-looking pair,* Annie thinks. Jean is wearing a soft purple dress and is looking younger and livelier already. She is blushing, of course, as she always does. They all gather in a group around the circulation desk. Even Stuart and Clare have come downstairs to join them.

"Jean, I can't wait for you to get back to work! The front desk isn't the same without you." Marie is gushing a bit, but that's fine.

Jean nods, smiling gratefully. They all chatter gaily, trying to make Jean feel at ease, while Duncan makes introductions all around.

"This is our cataloguer, Clare Draper, and our children's librarian, Stuart Cogswell—although their roles will soon be reversed, as the trustees have agreed to let them switch chairs." Duncan studiously avoids looking at Annie.

So that was it! Clare is letting Stuart have her job. That's what his new degree had been all about. Well, Stuart is certainly scrupulous and tidy enough for a cataloguer; maybe it will be a good thing. And Clare loves children almost as much as she loves stray dogs, so that will definitely be a good thing. But was this switch also the basis for their renewed relationship? Or is Stuart just using Clare's gullible nature to get her job, and then…what? Again, time will tell. And maybe Stuart will be too busy in his new job to go chasing Bella away, when she comes back.

"And this is Esa, who keeps this whole place ship-shape." Esa nods, smiling proudly. He is flushed and a little breathless after arriving through the back door, where he has been sweeping new-fallen snow off the steps and the ramp for handicapped.

"Oh, Miss Jean! Welcome back," Esa says. "We all missed ya!" Self-consciously, he gives her a handful of rumpled flowers—a few late purple pansies still blooming in the library garden, Annie suspects. "Here, I picked ya some vylets, Miss Jean; I know you lik'em. An' look, I foun' your pin, too, it must'a fallen off the day you got sick. I foun' it behind the trolley when I vacuumed, an' I kept it for ya."

"Oh, Esa, how sweet. Thank you!"

A patron is closing in on the group, curious about the cause of all the jollity. Duncan turns around and nods in recognition. He takes the patron gently by the elbow and pulls her into the circle.

"Well, hello, how nice to see you here today, Mrs. Ridley," he says, with slightly excessive politeness. "Mrs. Ridley is one of our most loyal patrons," he explains to Bentley and Stokes. "Oh, forgive me, Mrs. Ridley, you don't know everyone here. Let me introduce you. This is Mr. Bentley, and this is Mr. Stokes, Mr. Brian Stokes." Brian steps forward to shake her hand.

"Of course, I have heard *so* much about you, Mrs. Ridley. Delighted to make your acquaintance!" Brian says, smiling broadly, and Mrs. Ridley simply glows with pleasure at the attention.

ABOUT THE AUTHOR

Gunilla Caulfield was born and educated in Stockholm, Sweden, before immigrating to the United States. After ten years as an art dealer in Boston she moved to Rockport, a small fishing town and art colony on Cape Ann, *"That Other Cape,"* as they say on Cape Cod. She served as reference librarian at the Rockport Public Library, which is fictionally depicted in her mysteries. Along with husband Thomas and a steadily growing clan, she divides her time between Rockport, Massachusetts, and Bridgton, Maine.

Author webpage: *gunillacaulfield.com*

CPSIA information can be obtained at www.ICGtesting.com
Printed in the USA
LVOW101617231011
251710LV00018B/82/P